Doorways to the Unseen 6

6 Tales of Terror and Suspense

James Dermond

Ambages Books

ISBN: 978-1-946038-05-0

Cover art by Jeff Purnawan

"Her abode is concealed in the lowest recesses of a cave, wanting sun, and not pervious to any wind, dismal and filled with benumbing cold; and which is ever without fire, and ever abounding with darkness."

- 'Metamorphoses' by Ovid

Contents

Something in the Walls

S tanding in the tiled entryway, Timothy firmly shut the house door behind him. He inspected the front of a letter that had fallen through the door's mail slot, postmarked late last month. Addressed to him, the letter was from Eleanor Cooke, his stepsister who he hadn't seen since childhood. *What could Eleanor possibly want now,* Timothy thought, *after all these years?*

Timothy carefully slit the starch white envelope with an opener and read its contents:

Dear Tim,

I couldn't find your phone number or any other personal details among my mother's things besides this address. I hope this letter has gone to the right place and finds you well if it did.

You may think it strange that I've reached out to you after so many years of silence. I know that we were never close, mostly because of my mother, but something has transpired which has brought me home again.

Rose is afflicted from late-stage dementia and can no longer live on her own. She's been moved to a nursing facility where she can be cared for and I've taken conservatorship of her estate, including the family home. We played there in the yard together as children, for several summers.

But this is why I write to you: I've found something of your late father's that is quite interesting. Even intriguing. I can't say what it is other than that you must see it in person.

Over these last few years, my mother couldn't maintain the house as well as she should have, so I'm having it fully renovated by a local contractor. During the subsequent work, we found a feature in the home's cellar previously unknown to me. A feature your father most likely had knowledge of, based on what I found of his.

I'll be at 47 Grove Street during the daytime until renovations are complete, which the contractor estimates will be on May 27th. By the time this letter arrives, you should have several weeks to make the trip out-of-state and visit. But please call ahead so we can catch up and discuss your plans. Mother's home number is written on the back of this letter.

Cordially,

Eleanor

Timothy turned over the letter and saw a hastily written phone number. *I haven't seen Eleanor since we were probably ten years old,* Timothy mused to himself as he picked up the phone to call. The phone then rang for some time but there was no answer.

I'll just head down there tomorrow after checking in with the office, Timothy decided, wondering what his father may have left for him. *I don't want to waste any time...and I must see what's waiting for me.*

Picking up the phone again, Timothy called his brokerage. "Hello, Janice. I need to go out-of-town starting tomorrow. No, not too far. I'll be back on Monday. Please let David know he'll need to close the Sullivan property without me. And let him know I'll call Friday afternoon to make sure it went well."

I might even make an offer on the home, Timothy considered. *The market there is hot right now. But I won't broach the subject until I get ahold of whatever Eleanor has gotten from Dad.*

Involuntarily shuddering for a moment, Timothy recalled his stepmother's antiquated, sullen house and her cold, often imperious, manner. His memories of both were not good but, with the passage of time, he now held more impressions than actual recollections about the old place and Rose. But why had he suddenly become afraid? Timothy shrugged off the chill feeling and began to pack his suitcase for the next morning.

The trip along the expressway was a short one, leaving the bustle of the metro for the quiet, leafy environs of a historic city south along the coast. Timothy pulled his convertible sedan along a curb near the house on Grove Street, a two-story Georgian style frame dwelling, unremarkable in such a storied neighborhood. The house rested by itself in a wide alcove, twin chimneys protruding from its gray shingled roof, an open plot of elm trees nestled behind it.

A utility pickup truck and a silver sports coupe were parked against the street curb nearby, close to Timothy's car. Walking up the path to the house, Timothy reflected that the front door's ponderous, old-fashioned knocker could be something out of *A Christmas Carol*, the ghost of Jacob Marley about to speak his name as he reached for the brass doorknob. Finding it open, Timothy went inside, still half expecting the knocker to form a face and call out to him.

Construction work was being done somewhere in the house. The sound of a hammer pounding wood echoed as Timothy closed the door with a thud. He peered down the long hallway stretching before him from the house's foyer, rooms situated on either side, with no occupants in sight. Above the din of the laboring hammer, Timothy called out heartily: "Eleanor, it's me, Tim. I can't wait to see you! Are you there?"

A reply came from the parlor to the left, a woman's soft voice partly muffled by the noises in the house. "Yes, Timothy," the woman said. "Please, come into the drawing room. Make sure that the door is closed behind you."

As Timothy opened the cracked door, he saw a stylishly dressed young woman standing in the shadows near the fireplace. The parlor room's heavy lace curtains obscured most of the outside sunshine, but some daylight still filtered in through the windows onto the parlor floor, not reaching the room's corners. A folded pair of dark sunglasses and a glossy black portfolio were close at hand, both resting on a varnished wood table.

Eleanor smiled and stepped forward as Timothy shut the door tight, taking him by both arms as she leaned in to lightly kiss him on the cheek.

Surprised, Timothy rubbed the spot where Eleanor had given him a peck and then smiled in return. "We were just kids the last time we saw each other," Timothy noted, his grin quickly morphing into a smirk. "But you're all grown up now. I wasn't sure what to expect." Eleanor continued to smile but said nothing, her large, pale-blue eyes set against almost platinum hair, an icy blonde femme fatale.

"You've grown up as well, Tim," Eleanor replied after pausing to study his face, touching the side of his auburn hair flirtatiously. "The chubby boy from all those years ago turned out rather well. I'm glad you received my letter."

Timothy stood by a window and scanned the room in the half-light, the gilded portraits of Eleanor's forebearers seeming to dominate the space. Eleanor took a seat on a sofa and asked Timothy to join her. "Please sit down," she said brightly. "We've so much to discuss."

"Yes, indeed," Timothy agreed as he complied with her request. "But why all the mystery about my father's effects if that's all that you've found? And where did you find it, whatever it is?"

"We can talk about that later, upstairs," Eleanor indicated, reaching out to touch Timothy's arm again. "But what about yourself?" Eleanor inquired, her manner animated. "Are you married? Any children?"

Growing sheepish, Timothy turned away for a moment. "No, I've never been married," he replied dejectedly. "My work takes up so much of my time. But maybe the right girl will come along someday." Timothy suddenly hoped Eleanor was interested in him.

"And yourself?" Timothy asked, cheering. "Do you have a husband and children?"

"No," Eleanor said flatly, her reply oddly terse, followed by an awkward stillness between them.

"I've so more to tell you," Eleanor then declared, picking up the conversation again. "But first, down to business. I want to show you what Mr. da Silva found in the cellar before visiting your father's room."

Eleanor led Timothy down narrow steps, the top of his head almost touching the low plaster ceiling as they descended into the cellar. The cellar was cramped and unfinished but with conspicuously updated stained wood paneling installed along its walls.

Putting down a can of paint as Timothy and Eleanor stopped at the bottom of the steps, a stout, mustachioed man clad in overalls dusted off his palms and extended a greeting. "Fred da Silva," the man said, shaking Timothy's hand vigorously. "Ms. Cooke told me you might be coming."

"Timothy Faber," Timothy replied. "It's good to meet you." Looking past Mr. da Silva into a shadowy nook at the back of the cellar, Timothy observed a hefty pile of broken clay bricks close by.

Is that what we've come down here to see? Timothy wondered to himself as he scrutinized the debris. *It looks like they've discovered something unexpected down here.*

Eleanor stepped around the two men and stood by the shattered brick heap. "Mr. da Silva found this brick wall after knocking out some plaster to enlarge the cellar," Eleanor explained without looking at either of them. "He then bored into the wall as it seemed to be blocking another room in back. That's when we found the tunnel."

Coughing, Timothy stooped and investigated the dark recess. Through a gaping hole in the brick wall, a stone passage was faintly visible. The passage was wide enough to accommodate someone standing upright and seemed that it might lead to somewhere beneath the house.

"I told Ms. Cooke that it's probably an abandoned smuggler's tunnel," Mr. da Silva offered, reaching into one of the pockets of his overalls. "This house was no doubt built two centuries ago, but here's the thing: this brick wall and its plaster cover were put in much later, even just recently."

Producing a gold lighter and a red and green cigarette pack, Mr. da Silva pulled out a loose cigarette to place between his lips. "Mind if I smoke?" Mr. da Silva asked. "This house makes me nervous for some reason."

"No, go ahead," Timothy replied somewhat absent-mindedly as he squinted through the hole in the wall. As Mr. da Silva sparked its flame, Timothy noticed that his lighter was monogrammed with a bold *DS* on its engraved case.

"So, what are you going to do about this creepy tunnel?" Timothy queried as he turned to face Eleanor. "Can't you just seal it up again?"

"We could," Eleanor answered, "but Mr. da Silva thinks the tunnel might make the house's foundation structurally unsound. We should at least find out what's back there first. Where the tunnel leads to." The three of them stared at the aperture in the brick wall, an uneasy silence hanging in the air, the hole like an agonizing wound in the house itself.

"Tomorrow's another day, my friends," Mr. da Silva suddenly said, seeming to search the cellar for his paint can. "We can discuss what needs to be done in the morning. I need to close up shop and go home for the day."

Mr. da Silva nodded to Timothy as he put out his cigarette on a clay brick. "It was nice meeting you, Mr. Faber," he said, his smile weary but friendly. "Have a good evening."

Eleanor and Timothy watched as Mr. da Silva walked up the steps from the cellar, soon hearing a door close upstairs. "When did he find this tunnel, Eleanor?" Timothy questioned. "Do you think Mr. da Silva's right about it being used for nefarious undertakings, even if it was a long time ago?"

"I don't know," Eleanor replied distractedly, apparently unconcerned. "We found the brick wall and tunnel about a week ago. I sent you the letter right after we discovered it, hoping you'd turn up soon.

"I then told Fred to ignore the tunnel and to keep working on the rest of the house instead. He started back here just today." Eleanor glanced away to the steps exiting the cellar. "Come," she said. "Let's go upstairs."

Leading Timothy to the master bedroom, Eleanor opened the room's spacious closet and parted some clothes on hangers, reaching down as she did. After rummaging through a woven canvas trunk on the closet floor, Eleanor produced a slim, worn leather journal. Timothy took it in hand and began leafing through the journal's embrittled pages, yellowed, and creased with age.

"Be careful, Tim," Eleanor warned as he slowly flipped through the pages. "I suspect this journal is as old as the house itself. I found it at the bottom of a trunk of your father's belongings, soon after my mother went into the facility, but I didn't think much of it until Mr. da Silva found the tunnel. Now it makes more sense."

"How so?" replied Timothy, gingerly turning a page. "This just seems to be a personal diary but written in parts, using several different languages."

"Keep going and you'll see," Eleanor insisted. "I think it's actually written in a composite language, something like Esperanto, but even earlier. There are words derived from Greek, Latin, French, German, and some other languages I didn't recognize mixed in with numbers and symbols.

"And there are blank pages in the back," Eleanor then said in a low voice, her expression momentarily inscrutable. "The last entries could even be transcribed in invisible ink. The author wanted whatever the journal describes to be coherent only to a select few."

Timothy turned to the journal's final page and then looked at Eleanor, perplexed. "The author...who do you think wrote it?" he asked hesitantly, feeling baffled by the odd book.

"Elijah Cooke, my distant ancestor," Eleanor replied with almost unerring conviction, her eyes widening as her mouth formed into a broad grin. "The man who built this house. He made a fortune in shipping goods - maybe even contraband - into the plantation colonies and then used the money to fund this house's construction."

"But back to my point: what does this journal have to do with the tunnel downstairs?" Timothy questioned, his brow furrowing as he spoke. "You said it all makes sense now after finding the journal. How are the two connected, other than both are discomfiting relics of the past?"

Without answering, Eleanor turned to crouch and reached back into the canvas trunk, taking what looked like a map from a sturdy iron box. She then gave the map to Timothy as she put the box aside.

"Both the journal and this old map were in the metal box, the map folded up under the journal," Eleanor informed him, her tone eager, even slightly devious. "The box looks like it was locked at one time, but I was able to just open it. There's no key for the keyhole that I could find anywhere."

Timothy held the small paper map by its ends, the map's surface showing the outline of a network of labyrinthian tunnels. He was surprised that the aged map was still usable after so long, its fibers possibly strengthened with linen or flax.

"This map likely shows what was sealed off behind the brick wall," Eleanor said, half-trying to hide her excitement. "And, if so, the journal most assuredly describes what's hidden there.

"Fred believes there's another part of the cellar, below ground, but I think Elijah Cooke's lost treasure is buried somewhere in the tunnels sketched on the map. Long-standing rumors in provincial lore claimed something was secreted away beneath The Elijah Cooke House. And I think we've found it."

"It could be anything buried under the house, Eleanor," Timothy countered, suddenly worried about his stepsister. "What makes you believe there's a lost treasure here? This strange book could be anything as well: about alchemy, a kind of military code, or just pedantic gibberish."

"Elijah Cooke had dealings with smugglers, like I said, even pirates," Eleanor responded, irritated by Timothy's skepticism. "The pirates were supposed to have paid him in Spanish doubloons from the Caribbean. A cache of gold coins, worth millions, could just be waiting for us in those tunnels.

"The old man disappeared some years after the house was built," Eleanor continued, "after a deal with some of his less savory business associates may have gone sour, such as slavers. Or the pirates. Or both. But the house has remained in our family for all these generations, to this day."

"If the treasure's there, why not just go for it yourself?" Timothy asked, fearful he had brought himself into a dangerous situation. "You haven't seen me in years. I might as well be a stranger. Why trust me?"

"I've no one else to trust," Eleanor replied firmly, no longer seeming buoyant. "It's as simple as that. And I thought your father might have told you something about the map, in confidence."

"Never, Eleanor," Timothy answered. "No, not a word. Not that we ever spoke very much."

"Then you agree to help?" Eleanor asked, hopeful. "You'll help me? If there's nothing valuable there, we'll at least find out what's in those tunnels."

Timothy nodded, unsure, but also tempted by the allure of forgotten wealth, begging to be taken. *Who could say no?* Timothy reassured himself. *I can't.*

"Good," Eleanor said, once again upbeat. "Let's wait until Fred leaves tomorrow and then explore the tunnels. I'll bring flashlights and a lantern, and we'll take the map with us. Fred won't be back again until Monday morning, so we have enough time over the weekend to find our fortune, if there's one to be found."

Once downstairs, Timothy sat at the kitchen table and watched Eleanor take a can of coffee from the cupboard, running water into the coffee maker from the faucet. Fresh coffee began to percolate, Eleanor sitting down at the table to join him.

"It's so funny being back in the old house, after all these years," Timothy remarked as Eleanor gazed at him affectionately. He then paused before continuing, as if uncomfortable for a moment. "You know," Timothy confessed, "there were some nights here, nights while you were away at boarding school, that still haunt me."

Eleanor looked at Timothy quizzically, an expression of concern on her face. "How so?" she said urgently. "You're not trying to confess some past abuse you've kept secret until now, are you, Tim?" Eleanor seemed sad all the sudden, as if she were about to hear something she might have suspected about their childhood.

"No, nothing like that, Eleanor," Timothy replied hurriedly, upset by the suggestion. "I can assure you." Timothy then looked around the kitchen for a moment before speaking again, as if inspecting the room. "I've just always had a certain unease about this place, as did Dad. As if there was something in the walls of the house."

Without saying anything, Eleanor got up and poured two cups of coffee, returning to the table with the steaming mugs. "What do you mean?" Eleanor then inquired pointedly before taking a sip from her cup. "Like rats?"

Timothy drank from his mug and then looked back to Eleanor. "No, something else," he said, his voice becoming distant. "I could never quite explain it. If I didn't know any better, I could have sworn, more than once, that someone was behind my bedroom walls, moving around at night."

Eleanor took another sip from her coffee cup, as if unsure how to reply. "I don't really have any sharp memories of the house," Eleanor then declared, almost wistful as she said this. "But, then again, I can't even remember my own father. He died when I was very young, according to Mom; all I ever knew was your father, Tim. He was my real Dad, as much as I had one."

Eleanor lightly touched Timothy's hand and seemed about to say something. Instead, she took the last sip of her coffee and moved from the table to put the empty cup in the sink. "Have a good evening, stepbrother dearest," said Eleanor from the open arc of the kitchen doorway, ready to depart. "I'll see you tomorrow morning, bright and early at 8:00 a.m. Be back here for the treasure hunt after Fred leaves."

After dinner at a restaurant, Timothy checked into his hotel, some distance from Grove Street. The sun was beginning to set through the half-closed window blinds as he unlocked the door to his room, casting shadows over a neatly done-up single bed.

Sitting down to undress, Timothy thought back to his conversations with Eleanor that afternoon. Eleanor's mother had been largely absent from their lives after adolescence; even so, Rose never seemed 'quite there' to Timothy even as a boy. Her demeanor was often aloof when they were together with his father, as if she somehow resented his presence or even saw him as an intruder.

Night came but Timothy nevertheless lay awake, hazily recalling one afternoon at the old house many years ago. He hadn't thought of what had occurred that summer day since it happened but seeing Eleanor again had brought the memory back. He turned onto his side and shut his eyes tightly, the images of himself and Eleanor now as lucid as they were in their youthful pasts.

Eleanor sat in the shade of a blooming magnolia in the house's yard, her hands resting on her knees. She wore her requisite wide-brimmed sun hat and dark sunglasses, always on whenever she ventured outside. Rose insisted Eleanor remain covered up, the girl's milky complexion being quite sensitive according to her.

Perched atop his bicycle's striped leather seat, Timothy rode along the sidewalk, Eleanor watching him coast past the house's white picket fence. Without warning, Timothy abruptly lurched forward, sending him hurtling over the bike's handlebars and onto the hard pavement with a clamor.

Eleanor shot up from her spot and scanned the front of the house, removing her sunglasses as she did. Timothy staggered to his feet and opened the fence gate, forgetting his bike where it lay broken. He made his way to the house unsteadily, clutching a bloody elbow as he did.

"Tim!" Eleanor cried out after watching the scene unfold, then running to him from the sheltering tree, inspecting the arm he was grasping after she came to stand at his side. "You're bleeding," she observed. "Let me have a look."

Holding Timothy's damaged arm with both hands, Eleanor asked him to let her examine the wound. "How did it happen?" she asked, Timothy revealing a nasty gash across his left elbow. "You just went flying all of the sudden."

"I hit something; it got caught in the spokes," answered Timothy, wincing as Eleanor brought his arm closer to her face. "But I want to get some iodine on this cut before I find out what it was."

"Tim, your cheek's scraped pretty bad too," Eleanor said, her voice full of sympathy. Eleanor stood on her tips of her saddle shoes, kissing Timothy on the cheek in a place where he hadn't been hurt. As she stepped back, Eleanor saw a thin drop of blood forming in the open abrasion, as if it might stream down Timothy's chin.

Almost unconsciously, she reached up to catch the droplet on her finger, then licking the fresh blood from her fingertip in one fluid motion. Timothy stared into Eleanor's face as he saw this, a perverse look of satisfaction now resting there.

"Why did you do that?" Timothy asked uneasily, putting a hand to the scrape as if to search for more blood from his injury.

"Do what?" Eleanor replied, apparently surprised at the question. "Oh, you mean...I don't know, it just seemed like the right thing to do."

***

Sleep eventually took hold of Timothy and the night passed into the morning. Rolling over, Timothy squinted at the table flip clock's blocky white numbers, displaying 9:27 a.m. He had slept in, despite requesting a wakeup call from the front desk the prior evening.

"Why didn't I get a wakeup call?" The young man behind the lobby's counter turned to see who was speaking to him. "I'm sorry, sir," he told Timothy. "What room are you staying in?" The hotel clerk attempted to hide his irritation at Timothy's brusque manner but was entirely unsuccessful at doing so.

"I'm staying in Room 372," Timothy replied. "I checked in yesterday evening when there was a different person behind the desk. Did I get a call or not?" Timothy waited for an answer, taking another gulp from his vending machine paper cup.

"You did, sir," the clerk said after checking a logbook under the counter. "I placed the call myself several hours ago. The phone rang and rang but there was no reply. I apologize if there was any inconvenience."

His head dull and throbbing, Timothy drove back to where Eleanor was waiting for him, he hoped. He had phoned the house from his hotel room, but no one had taken the call. *Eleanor may have just been down in the cellar with Mr. da Silva*, Timothy thought to himself, cursing his heavy slumber.

Why had he slept so deeply, failing to answer a ringing phone, even one next to his bed? *There had been a nightmare last night after I finally fell asleep*, Timothy thought. *Something that put me down. But I can't remember what it was now.*

The door to the house was unlocked again. Mr. da Silva's truck and Eleanor's silver coupe were both parked nearby, as Timothy had expected. Once inside, he found two cups of coffee cooling on the kitchen table, having been poured recently and then left unfinished.

So, they must be downstairs, Timothy thought. *That's why Eleanor didn't answer the phone. I just hope they didn't decide to go into the tunnels without me.* Timothy walked down into the cellar, finding the space as it had been left the previous day, but empty.

But next to the brick wall lay Mr. da Silva's bag of tools, which he had left in the kitchen the day before. *It seems da Silva may have put the bag here so he could crawl through,* Timothy decided. *I'm glad I wore jeans for this.*

Timothy pulled himself into the exposed opening in the brick wall, the dark tunnel ahead. Running his hand over its walls after standing upright, the tunnel's masonry work appeared like that of the house above, the stones having been laid in colonial times. Timothy turned on the flashlight he had taken from da Silva's tool bag and then stepped into darkness, the solitary beam of light revealing the way ahead.

At the far end of the tunnel were piles of large rocks, having been cleared away to make whatever was below accessible. The entire tunnel appeared to have been blocked with the worn mass of rocks and then unsealed at some point, its reason untold.

The stone passage descended at an incline, quickly becoming earthen instead. Near the passage's bottom were yet more earthen passages, leading in several different directions. *Eleanor's map likely shows what's down here, but I don't have it,* Timothy reflected. *Should I turn around and call the police? They might be hurt, so I shouldn't waste any more time. I need to find them.*

The passage south was much deeper than Timothy had anticipated, continuing for some time but with no sign of either Mr. da Silva or Eleanor. The passage then veered to what Timothy thought was east, taking steps down its path until he noticed the glint of metal somewhere on the passage floor. It was Mr. da Silva's monogrammed lighter, its stylized "DS" visible after brushing off the dirt encrusting it.

They must be close, Timothy decided. *I just hope they're alright.* The eastern passage emerged into a chamber of sorts, its rounded corners partially filled with what appeared to be bones. At the other end of the chamber was a figure, slouching in the dim light of Timothy's flashlight.

The figure's mummified remains were clothed upon examination, this poor unfortunate having been manacled to the chamber wall at the time of his demise. Timothy shined his light aside, a pile of rags and broken chains within reach of the prisoner. An inscription, crudely hewed, was carved into the nearby wall's soft stone.

So, I have been taken captive. The creatures that dwell here, cousins of Mankind from before our History, have acted with the aid of human conspirators, in the hopes I might reveal where my Wealth has been sequestered away. I have told them nothing, so they leave me here to rot out of spite.

At first, I befriended these strange beings, living here in this light-less place, hidden from Christ's Mercy. I learnt to speak their peculiar tongue, informing them of the world above this one. They slowly became more demanding, asking for meat. For flesh of the most repulsive variety. And captives. Women. For an unspeakable purpose I dare not discuss.

Had I realized the creatures' domain was under this plot, I would have never built my Manse here among the groves. My prayer to Our Lord is that these Ungodly Monstrosities be sealed off, so no harm can come to His Servants now that they know of us.

Another glimmer of metal reflected Timothy's flashlight beam, from beneath the rags. Parting the decomposing tatters with a foot, Timothy spied a small music box lying on its side.

Carefully, Timothy opened the bejeweled box. The box's lid unlatched, a ballerina began to pirouette on her tiny pedestal, a sweet melody echoing in the otherwise silent chamber. Momentarily spellbound by the haunting cadence of the notes, Timothy's thoughts turned inward, to the disturbing night terror from his sleep, a suppressed phantasm of a storm swept night spent at the old house years ago.

The dim thumping in the walls had returned, prodding Timothy from his slumber. Timothy wasn't sure what he had heard the night before but, this time, it was clear. Something was in the walls, moving about behind this bed. Sitting up, Timothy heard the noises stop.

Lightning flashed outside the bedroom window and there was a clap of thunder. Timothy's father, Rupert, was again away on business, and Timothy was alone in the house with Rose for a second night. He had searched for Rose earlier in the evening, even checking the cellar door which remained locked shut as it had always been. Assuming she was downstairs, Timothy went to bed despite the din from the terrible storm brewing.

A jewel-encrusted music box rested on a dresser past the bed's footboard, its lid closed. Timothy roused himself and stood in front of the bedroom window, reaching up to take the music box as more thunder rumbled faintly in the distance. Opening the antique device, an exquisite porcelain dancer posed in the box's center, soft music now chiming as the ballerina turned.

Teeming rain splattered the glass of the window. Timothy listened as he heard a door open from the floor below, then close. 'That sounded like the cellar door,' Timothy thought. 'Why would Rose have been down there all this time?'

He shut the box's cover and climbed back into bed. There were footsteps outside his door, which paused at the threshold. The footsteps then resumed, trailing off, their sound quieted by the tumultuous thunderstorm. His head on his pillow, Timothy drifted into sleep.

He soon woke again, rolling waves of cracking and booming thunder pulling Timothy into an uncertain wakefulness. Rose was at the foot of the bed, partially concealed by the hanging canopy. She stared at Timothy without uttering a word, the rank odor of rotted meat assaulting Timothy's nostrils.

There, in the darkness of the bedroom, a hunched form stood behind Rose. It heaved in shallow, ragged breaths, the smell of the thing's foul gasps acrid and pungent. A mercurial lightning streak revealed for but a moment something that appeared like an albino ape, then the room once again was almost devoid of light.

With Rose, the creature turned to leave through the open door, the crashing tempest outside nearly shaking the house. The door to the bedroom closed behind them and Timothy fell back into sleep, his semiconscious mind unsure if what he had seen was truly real or yet another nightmare.

There was a noise from down the passage to the chamber, a yowl, or the cry of a feral animal. Searching for an exit, Timothy noticed another tunnel leading away and took it.

He stumbled through the egress passageway, hearing more cries and wails coming from behind him, the light from his flashlight casting over loose stones and aberrant foot tracks left in the dreck by this underworld's putrescent inhabitants.

The choked passages twisted and turned, one soon becoming indistinguishable from the next. The relentless primal yowling grew closer, almost palpable, and now Timothy was all but lost in this seemingly endless underground maze.

He spied a glow in the distance, at the passage's end, the kind of light that might come from a lamp. Timothy went to the light instinctively, his overpowering fright blotting out why he had descended into these accursed tunnels to begin with.

A lantern was set on the ground of this open chamber, its dim blue radiance illuminating a grisly scene not far away. Eleanor knelt over Mr. da Silva's corpse, slurping and gobbling, her back arched to Timothy's view.

Coming closer, Eleanor snapped around, her long silvery hair wild, her mouth and teeth smeared with bright red gore from da Silva's half-eaten face. Standing, Eleanor slowly walked to Timothy, her head low, the color of her eyes now a dull, greyish scarlet.

Timothy desired to flee but was paralyzed with fear; he was frozen in place as if a great force held him there. Eleanor took a crimson-stained hand and slid it under Timothy's chin, leaning in as if to kiss his cheek. Timothy's blood-curdling screams echoed from the walls of the subterranean passageways and tunnels, answered only by the primordial shrieks of Eleanor Cooke's bestial kindred.

The Dining Car at Midnight

What a miserable little town, Charles decided, grimacing as he noted the hovel homes around him. Having just left the ill-maintained docks where the ferry had deposited its fares, Charles was tired after his long river trip. He had walked some distance with his luggage before placing the suitcases down on the cobblestones of what appeared to be the town center. Charles saw that there were few other travelers thereabouts, the dusky locals conspicuous from any visitors due to their gaudy clothing and dubious manner.

Checking his suit coat for his ticket and then glancing at his pocket watch, Charles considered how much time he had before taking his leave. *The train depot shouldn't be too far from here. And I still have a few hours before departure. But I shouldn't want to eat lunch in this place.*

He picked up his suitcases by their handles and spied signage not far away. The signs were not in a language he could easily translate, but it was clear from the peeling building's façade from which the signs dangled that this was the railway station.

The waiting train on the station's tracks consisted of seven cars and a locomotive with its attached coal bin, all of which were of contemporary design. Sleek and outwardly luxurious, the modern-day transport posed a sharp contrast to the environs of this sleepy, out-of-the-way burgh where it was now parked. After spending the last several months first at sea and then at an Oriental capital, Charles was pleased to see something recognizable, a reminder of the Pullman cars from his cross-country travels at home.

The connecting passengers must still be on the train, Charles thought as he stepped onto the mostly vacant station platform, momentarily excited at the notion of joining them onboard. *The next ferry won't dock until late this afternoon. This town isn't exactly welcoming to outsiders, so I don't blame them for remaining where they are for now.*

An ominous-seeming carriage was pulled up not far from the railroad station, near to the train's rearmost baggage car, two charcoal-black horses hitched to its front. The four-wheeled carriage's style was that of a bygone era, antiquated, but with a velvety case and plush interior still richly textured and opulent. A flatbed wagon also drawn by two horses was being driven away nearby, leaving the train station, rolling over the cobbled streets.

Charles watched as the train's porters loaded a large wooden crate into the rear baggage car, struggling under its considerable weight. A gloved man wearing a felt bowler hat closely observed them. He then noticed Charles, giving him a bewildering smile as he did. The man almost leered at Charles, as if he were about to suggest something quite lurid to him.

Boarding the train, Charles handed his ticket to the assistant conductor, who waited at the car's passenger entrance. He was directed to his assigned sleeping accommodations, where he would ride in a single compartment.

Charles noted the compartment's darkly elegant, lacquered wood and inlaid marquetry as he opened its door. A small washstand was near the berth, which was folded into a seat for the time being. *The splendor of this train compares to that of the finest hotels*, Charles reflected, *either at home or here abroad*.

A three-course lunch was being served in the dining car. Charles strolled to the restaurant, finding the train somewhat empty for its lengthy cross-border trek back to its home station. The *maître d'hôtel* greeted Charles as he stood in the dining car's threshold, his trim mustache wrinkling as he inspected his latest guest.

"Will you be dining alone, *Monsieur*?" The head waiter inquired, an inkling of derision in his tone. "There are tables for solo travelers, or you may sit with other passengers if you wish. Our entrée this afternoon is chicken 'à la chasseur, with oysters as the appetizer."

Looking around the partially unoccupied coach, Charlies noticed an older couple seated nearby, a man and his wife. The man noticed Charles with the waiter and waved him over, as if encouraging him not to dine by himself.

"I can sit with the man and his lady, if you don't mind," Charles replied, gesturing toward the distinguished pair. "They seem to want company."

"You shouldn't have to eat all by yourself," the man said as Charles sat across from him. "We've plenty of room here. We were just about to order lunch." The man smiled genially at Charles, his wife smiling as well but staying silent.

"My name's Charles Hubbard," Charles said, extending his hand to greet the man. "I'm a senior correspondent for *The Daily Sentinel* newspaper. We're planning to open an overseas news bureau later this year. I'll be the new bureau's first editor-in-chief."

The man shook Charles' hand vigorously. "Sir Andrew Saxton," the man said in reply. "And this is my dearest wife, Winifred. We're on our maiden trip aboard this new luxury line. Isn't it just exquisite?"

"Yes, I'm quite impressed," Charles remarked as his eyes searched for a waiter. "Even more so as my employer is footing the bill for all of this. But why didn't you offboard for the ferry at our last station?"

"Winifred and I haven't left the train since our departure last week," Sir Andrew answered. "We're getting on in years and didn't want to traverse the final, rough part of the journey by boat. What I really wanted to see was this region, so steeped in history as it is."

Charles suddenly became curious. "Really? How so? I thought this place had always been a backwater, removed from most of the great events of the past."

"Not quite," Sir Andrew corrected. "Kings and queens have graced these remote lands; an order of crusading knights even kept a garrison here. That is, before their Grand Master was burned at the stake for heresy, among other things."

"Heresy?" Charles inquired. "Like what? Did he deny the existence of God or something?" Charles found the notion a quaint one.

"No, not entirely," Sir Andrew said, the timbre of his voice lowering as he spoke. "The Grand Master was purported to have claimed that he was a half-daemon, and that through the ritual drinking of human blood, he would someday fully attain eternal life, even godhood."

Sir Andrew continued. "But he and his Order were put to an end by the King. He was said to have cursed the King and his line before his execution by fire, pledging to someday rise from the grave, restore his Order, and take his revenge against those who had wronged him. The Grand Master's surviving acolytes were then reputed to have spirited away his charred remains following his immolation by royal decree."

Surprised by this macabre turn in the conversation, Charles was startled when a waiter approached their table and asked if they wished to order lunch. Charles said yes but wanted to hear more from Sir Andrew before he ate anything.

"This curse, did something ever come of it?" Charles was almost starting to give credence to this story; Sir Andrew was so convincing as he related it.

"Yes, if the legends are to be believed," Sir Andrew now wore an enigmatic expression across his face. "The King who sentenced the knights and their master to a fiery death died himself soon after. The King's death was supposed to have been a hunting accident, but from the account of witnesses, the King had died of a terrible fright instead."

Lunch came, and Charles took a small bite from his cooked chicken after slicing a piece off with his table knife. Sir Andrew and Winifred, still silent, ate the same meal. Charles' curiosity concerning this esoteric knightly brotherhood hadn't waned. He then asked, "Does this order still exist? I mean, do you know if the heirs of those knights have a fraternal society today?"

"I believe they may," Sir Andrew replied, his voice strangely quiet. "But if the Order continues on, its members maintain themselves in secret."

There was an uneasy break in the conversation following this remark, with Sir Andrew suddenly excusing himself. "I'm going to take a cigar on the vestibule. It was good meeting you, Mr. Hubbard. I hope we meet again soon." Sir Andrew stood and walked away, Winifred offering an almost whispered goodbye to Charles as she followed her husband out of the dining car.

Finishing his meal after a while, Charles then rose and entered the car vestibule where Sir Andrew had stood only moments ago, briefly glancing at Charles' table through the open doorway before slipping off. The aroma of cigar smoke still hung over the now empty space, its distinctivefragrance sharp and sweet. Charles ambled toward his compartment near the back of the train, intent on getting some writing done prior to dinner.

***

It was night, the evening coming sooner than expected. Charles sat alone in his compartment, watching the nighttime forest's densely knotted boles pass by his window under the moonlight. The train had left what little civilization existed in this part of the world, journeying into a yawning woodland darkness.

Charles had started drafting what would eventually be a multi-part article for *The Daily Sentinel*, covering his recent transcontinental adventure and the politics of the foreign country he had visited. *The Mustafa hopes to pull his hidebound compatriots into this century*, Charles mused to himself, putting away his journal and writing pen.

The hour was late, but Charles decided to venture outside his compartment and visit the adjoining baggage car, with the mystery cargo hoisted into it earlier in the day. He thought back to the unsettling man on the station platform and his weird, unnerving smile.

I wonder if the crate might have been pried opened by the porters. I'd bet they'd be as curious as I am about the thing. Charles stood in the narrow passage outside his compartment and made his way to the rear car's gangway connection. He paused for a moment in the tight vestibule and then heaved open the baggage car's iron-bound door.

A hanging lantern swayed from the car's arched ceiling, throwing shark shadows about the crowded freight room as Charles teetered under the train's movement. Heavy boxes lined the walls of the car, with scores of passengers' luggage on either side of a tapering path ending at a bulky crate resting toward the car's back.

Charles stopped in front of the crate and looked up, examining its sides. Unfamiliar script was stamped along the crate's wood surface, with some numbers near its top that seemed to indicate a shipping schedule. Reaching out to run a hand over the crate's paneling, Charles abruptly pulled back once he touched his palm to its surface.

The crate is so cold...unnaturally cold, Charles thought as he shivered, warming his hand in a coat pocket. *The crate feels as if it's been left outside in winter.* As Charles looked around the car, he noticed his breath had begun to frost, revealing a thin mist as he nervously exhaled.

The train car shifted unexpectedly, and the ponderous crate groaned, sliding slightly along the floorboards. Charles felt a shadow behind him, the tenebrous form's drawn fingers seeming to reach for Charles as the shadow grew longer, stretching over the crate.

Charles turned, and the shadow receded, with only the sounds of the creaking lantern and the train clattering on its track apparent. Afraid, Charles began to hurry towards the car's door when he heard a noise outside in the vestibule.

Entering, he saw the back of a man in a funereal coat and hat, pulling shut the door to the connecting passenger coach. Charles stepped forward, and the man turned to him, surprised. It was the man in the bowler hat from the station platform.

"Sir, what is your business in the luggage compartment at this hour?" The man queried, his voice as unpleasant as his visage. "You should be in your room, asleep."

"I could ask you the same, sir," Charles replied with some menace. "Now, let me be on my way. Please, step aside."

The two men passed each other in the compact space, wary and facing one another. Now that Charles was close, he could see that the man had a bloodless complexion, with bruised circles under both of his eyes.

The man leered at Charles again for a moment as he passed and then quickly busied himself with the door to the baggage car. From the corner of his eye, Charles saw the man close the baggage car door behind himself as he exited the vestibule.

Returning to his sleeping quarters, Charles rested on the open berth after hanging his necktie. The light in his compartment slowly dimmed, and Charles drifted into a languid slumber, lulled to sleep by the moving train.

Charles dreamt of a bleak and inhospitable place, barren and desolate save for a black fortress resting against the side of a jagged and broken mountain. Up a path to the mountain assembled a solemn procession, bearded men holding aloft banners and wearing tunics that displayed an inverted cross.

The procession entered the magnific stronghold, carrying a bronze coffin to a resting place within. A horrifically burnt corpse was removed from the coffin and lowered into a stone pool filled with blood, soon restoring what was once a man to a semi-living state. The awful creature made a sinister laugh as it stood upright in the viscous crimson ichor, triumphant at having conquered death itself.

Drifting in and out of his fitful sleep, Charles felt intense, burning eyes on him before finally awakening to a lightless compartment. He sat up on his berth and heard footsteps outside his door, noticeable in the otherwise quiet train at midnight.

Cautiously, Charles turned the compartment's doorknob and stepped into the hallway outside his room. It was empty. More footsteps echoed from somewhere at the end of the sleeping car's passage, and Charles decided to follow them.

It may be that ghoulish man from the freight carriage, spying on me, Charles concluded. *I won't let him get away!*

The footsteps continued until Charles reached the dining car, the door to the restaurant cracked open. The sweet, sharp tang of Sir Andrew's cigar smoke wafted through the vestibule, seemingly to trail from within the car itself.

Was it Sir Andrew then? thought Charles. *Perhaps a late-night snack?* But the dining car was as dark as the rest of the train at this hour.

The overhead gas lamps of the restaurant car seemed to light themselves as Charles entered. At each of the dining tables were guests, men and women, impeccably dressed for a formal occasion. They smiled all at once: their fangs bared, their lips ruby-red against pale white, cadaverous skin.

The door behind Charles closed silently, and the guests rushed forward, swarming him, cutting off a scream of terror before it left Charles' throat. They fed voraciously from Charles' now still form, ceasing only after the last drop of blood was consumed.

***

The porter knocked twice before unlocking the door to Charles' compartment with his key. "Is anyone here?" the porter asked heedfully as he turned the doorknob. "The train's stopped, and you're the last passenger to not claim any baggage. You must disembark at this station."

Charles' drained and anemic corpse lay on his berth, his glassy eyes open and staring. The porter stood over Charles, deciding that he had died in his sleep a few nights ago and no one had noticed. But what was peculiar was that Charles was fully dressed, except for his necktie.

Badcock's Tonic Bitters

"Come one, come all! Come and see the amazing cure-all tonic, truly a miracle of modern medicine." As he spoke, Benjamin Badcock held a bottle of bluish liquid in the air, about the size of a whiskey flask, allowing the crowd to get a better look at his product. Dozens of townspeople had gathered around the raised stage in front of Badcock's horse-drawn wagon, gawking at the snake-oil salesman. A cloth-covered stand on the wood platform displayed four of the bottles in a line, with the sign underneath reading *Badcock's Tonic Bitters*.

The town of Tabletop was nestled among the foothills of a large and arid plane, in the shadows of a mesa overlooking the town. This barren rock formation provided shade to the town's inhabitants from the strong sun on the frontier, allowing the noon rays to be at least bearable. Badcock had rolled into Tabletop around this time and had set up shop, new to the community.

Babcock scanned his eyes along the faces before him. "You, young man," shouted Badcock into the assembled throng upon reaching someone toward the back. "Are you afflicted by any ailment? I saw that you limped as you walked to the stage. Do you have the gout?"

Tall and lean, and wearing a cattleman's hat, the young man answered with some emotion, "I was thrown from a horse awhile back and my leg's still not quite right. You're sayin' that your liniment can fix that?"

"Indeed, my good friend," Badcock replied. "Indeed, I am. Please step up here and be the first to buy a phial of Badcock's Tonic Bitters, at the knock down price of only one dollar. Truly a bargain for such a wonderous concoction!"

The man in back stepped onto the stage as the crowd parted, moving stiffly as he did. Removing a single dollar from a billfold, Badcock exchanged a bottle from his display stand for the solitary note. The cattleman took only a swallow of the elixir at first, which was then followed by a gulp, taking the rest down in one guzzle.

The man rubbed his bad leg and said, "I think it's gettin' better. It don't feel so sharp no more." He then began to walk around the stage more confidently, until his limp disappeared after several steps.

"I'm cured!" the man exclaimed. "My leg's as good as new. This here tonic done did it!" He then slapped Badcock on the back, almost knocking off his barker's top hat, and beamed to the gathering from the stage.

The townspeople immediately rushed forward, waving dollar bills, vying to be the first to buy a bottle of the magic tonic. Badcock took a full case of the stuff out from behind his stand, opening the box and grabbing customers' one-dollar notes as they were hastily handed to him.

"Remember, my good friends," Badcock announced as he sold the last bottle from the case. "The results may take some time. Give it a few days to cure what ails you. Badcock's Tonic Bitters is your one-and-only antidote for aches and pains."

Later, in the early evening, as the burnt-orange sun set over the high desert prairie, Badcock drove his wagon to the outskirts of the town. The man in the cattle hat rested against a sparse tree in the twilight, the embers of a lit cigar revealing his presence in the semi-dark.

Badcock patted the flank of his horse after dropping down from the wagon's seat, walking to its back end past the stylized letters painted on its side, *The Medicine Show*. Reaching into the wagon, Badcock produced a paper box from which he took a stack of dollar bills. The cattleman was already at his side, waiting.

"Try not to topple the hat from my head next time," Badcock insisted as he handed his accomplice his cut of the take. "There was no need for all those theatrics."

"I just wanted to make it look real, that's all," the man replied, squinting as he counted the notes in the low light. "It looks like we made out this time."

"Yes, indeed we did," Badcock said, smiling in the dark. "We'll meet next in Cortez, three days from now. Show up the day before as always, so it's not too suspicious."

The cattleman grinned and pocketed his loot, tipping his hat, and then made his way to a horse hitched to the nearby tree. Badcock climbed into the back of the wagon, inspecting his remaining cases of the tonic. What he had in stock should last him for at least the next several towns on this trip, if not more.

Badcock's wagon rolled on over the solitary road out-of-town, a lone traveler on this otherwise deserted rocky pathway. There was a sharp snapping sound beneath him and Badcock lurched forward in his seat as the wagon abruptly shifted to one side.

Damn, it's that wheel again, Badcock cursed. *It might be broken for sure this time.*

Badcock let himself down from the lopsided wagon and strained his eyes in the moonlight. The spokes of one of the wheels in back had caught on something in the dark, splintering them, and bringing his journey to a halt. The wheel's rim was wedged into the dirt, no longer capable of turning without outside intervention.

Letting out a sign, Badcock stepped of the pitted road and into the sparse grass beyond it, the occasional tree dotting the fields the only shelter. He unbuttoned the fly of his trousers and began to relieve himself against one of the trees, its leaves rustling softly in the night-time breeze.

Whistling a tune as he faced the tree trunk, Badcock failed to hear someone approach his wagon on the road from Tabletop.

"Turn around with your hands up, you no-good cheat," the thin, reedy voice commanded in short gasps. "You poisoned me with your charlatan's brew."

Slowing facing the road as he buttoned his pants, Badcock saw the silhouette of a man holding a revolver, the gun's barrel pointed at him. The bearded man slouched as he stood on the road, clutching his stomach with his free hand as if in pain, but still was able to keep his gun trained on Badcock.

"Why, my good sir, I did no such thing," Badcock insisted with rehearsed sincerity, taking a step forward as he put up his hands. "I'm sure if you believe I've harmed you in some manner, we can reach an amiable solution. I'm more than willing to compensate you appropriately for any malfeasance."

"That's enough, not one foot closer," the old miner wheezed, his firearm shaking slightly. "What I want is an antidote if you got one. If you ain't got a cure, I'll shoot you where you stand. Your days a sellin' quack remedies will be through."

"You must have had a bad reaction, that's all," Badcock assured the man, mentally calculating how quickly he could pull his pocket derringer from under his jacket sleeve once he drew near his assailant. "I keep a tincture of laudanum in the back of my wagon for just such a purpose. If you would allow me to fetch it for you..."

Keeping his hands in the air, Badcock motioned as if to take a step toward the wagon. The miner shallowed in agony and then waved his gun, beckoning Badcock to him.

"No tricks now, I've got you in my sights," the miner warned as he took aim once again, his voice almost fading with the last word.

Badcock relaxed his arms and reached for a small chest, resting among some crates. The miner observed him carefully, his breathing now shallow and uneven.

The chest did hold a tincture of laudanum, but Badcock had no intention of sharing any of it with this dying fool. But before he could take the chest in hand, the old miner was suddenly seized by a spasm, his firing arm reflexively dropping to his side.

Seeing his chance, Badcock rapidly reached for the Colt derringer in its custom sleeve holster, sliding the gun into his hand with ease.

The miner raised his head after doubling over and saw the bullet discharge, striking him squarely in the chest. He stumbled backward and fell, but not before firing a return round into Badcock's gut.

Badcock sank to the ground, leaning on the wagon's back. The dark sky above him grew blurred but not before he saw a man's face peer down at him.

***

"I wasn't sure if you were going to make it." The voice from the darkness sounded muffled to Badcock, as if it was being filtered through a heavy gauze. "You were out for more than a day after I extracted the bullet. But you should recover in time."

The room was sunlit, Badcock's eyes adjusting to the sudden intrusion of daylight. He rolled his head on the pillow and saw what looked like the shelves of a surgery, lined with glass jars filled of bandages and other medicinal supplies. The man standing over Badcock appeared friendly, his avuncular mustache and gentle smile reassuring him.

"I was shot," Badcock noted from his pillow, fatigued, and still feeling dizzy.

"That you were, my friend," his host affirmed, turning away to reach for something on a shelf. "But your disgruntled customer wasn't so lucky. Was he wanting a refund?"

"Not exactly." Badcock tried to sit up on the surgery table but then felt a stabbing pain in his midsection. He lay back down, resting on his back, an unlit gaslight lamp hanging over him from the ceiling.

"Well, you can tell me more about it later," the man said, speaking from the threshold of the doorway, just out of sight. "Just rest up. We should be able to move you to a proper bed in a day or two. I'll be back with some water from the well."

Badcock closed his eyes, listening to footsteps echo down the hallway and then an exterior door creak open. Without realizing it, he fell again into sleep, despite the rays of sunlight covering his face.

***

A few days had passed before Doc Loveless relocated Badcock to a guest bedroom upstairs in his home. The doctor's surgery was in the same house, which is where the doctor saw all his patients. Doc Loveless had told Badcock he was only medical doctor within the immediate vicinity of Tabletop; the next closest doctor was hours away by carriage.

A night shirt over his freshly changed dressing, Badcock sat up in bed and hungrily ate his lunch of watery oatmeal in a bowl. He was beginning to gain some of his strength back after the ordeal on the road outside of town, even though he could barely eat because of his stomach wound.

Knocking from behind the partially open door, Doc Loveless called out pleasantly, "Can I come in, Benjamin?" The bright sun pouring in through the bedroom window made Badcock shield his eyes with a hand before answering.

"Yes, please do." Badcock put aside the bowl and its porcelain serving tray as Doc Loveless walked to the foot of the brass railed bed, his black doctor's bag in hand.

"What's my prognosis, Doc?" Badcock asked intently. "It looks like I'm going to live, but how long until I'm healed up?" Badcock didn't feel he was in danger, but he also had no actual idea of where he was. He had never heard of a Doctor Mortimer Loveless during his visit to Tabletop and now feared the town marshal might be looking for him.

"Mortimer, please," replied casually without answering the question, looking into his bag as he did. "I'm on a first name basis with all my patients."

Doc Loveless produced a strange device, a kind of wooden cylinder with a hole bored into either end. He adjusted his bifocal lenses and then tilted his head, putting one end of the device to his ear.

"Is that some kind of wood seashell, Doc? I mean, Mortimer" inquired Badcock mirthfully. "I don't think you'll be able to hear the ocean from where we're at. We're landlocked."

"No, Benjamin," Doc Loveless said calmly. "It's a relatively new medical aid. Now, please open your night shirt. I'm going to check to your heartbeat for any irregularities."

Without further comment, Badcock opened his shirt and let Doc Loveless listen to his heart beating, breathing steadily. After a few minutes, he put away the mahogany cylinder, Doc Loveless seeming to be satisfied.

"You're very fortunate, Benjamin," Doc Loveless pronounced. "Old Clem's bullet nearly went clean through, without major damage to the intestines. I believe the risk of infection to be low as of this time."

Doc Loveless adjusted his glasses again as he gazed upward, a mannerism of his associated with a moment of reflection. "We only need to keep sanitizing the wound regularly until it's fully healed. I'll remove the sutures I put in around then."

"But how long?" asked Badcock again. "I mean, I'm grateful for you putting me up, even saving my life, but I've got people to meet and a business to run."

Doc Loveless cleared his throat for a moment. "A month, perhaps longer," he answered, looking over at a calendar on the guest bedroom wall. "Bullet wounds to the stomach are among the most egregious injuries. You could have very well died out on that road if I hadn't been riding into town that night."

Badcock grimaced as he heard the news. "What about Old Clem, if that was the man's name?" Badcock asked, seemingly slightly dazed as he spoke, then paused. "I killed a man...something I had never done before, so help me. But I swear it was in self-defense."

"That's what it appeared to me," Doc Loveless said. "No one will give a thought about Old Clem or go looking for him. The good people of Tabletop knew he was a drunkard and a troublemaker. But he seemed to think you had wronged him somehow. Did you?"

Badcock replied, "He was a customer like you said, from earlier that day. He bought a bottle of *Badcock's Tonic Bitters,* and it didn't sit right with him. It's strong stuff, a 'cure-all tonic' as I say in my pitch to the crowds."

"What's the tonic made of, Benjamin?" asked Doc Loveless inquisitively, seeming to be more than mildly curious. "Could Clem really have been badly sick because of your tonic?"

"I doubt it," Badcock answered hesitantly, suggesting he was unsure himself. "But like I said, it's strong medicine, and the cure can sometimes be worse than the ailment."

Looking around nervously as if confused, Badcock then asked, "Where's my wagon? My goods and inventory, are they safe? That's my entire livelihood in that wagon."

"Your wagon is safe," Doc Loveless assured him. "I was able to unstick your wheel and get the wagon out of the road. It's secured behind this residence right now." Badcock exhaled but said nothing, not fully certain his goods were fine, even after Doc Loveless' explanation.

"Alright then," Doc Loveless said, ending the conversation with a pat on Badcock's shoulder. "I'll leave you to rest. And let me take that tray for you. Dinner will be after 6:00 p.m. this evening. Yet more oatmeal I'm afraid."

The evening came soon, with the sun slowly setting outside of Badcock's window, leaving the room dark except for the moonlight on its windowsill. Badcock hadn't left the house since his arrival, using a basin supplied and emptied every day by Doc Loveless to relieve himself instead of venturing to the outhouse. He could barely walk in his condition as it is.

Where's dinner? thought Badcock urgently, wishing Loveless would at least come in to turn on the dresser in the room's gas lamp. Badcock suddenly realized that he had neither seen nor heard anyone else in the house except for Doc Loveless; the doctor had yet to mention a wife and children or even other patients. Were there any?

Hours passed, the moon becoming clouded over, the waning moonlight from the outside the window creating an eerie shadow world within the spacious bedroom. Badcock knew that he could walk if he needed to, as he had made it up the stairs to the house's second floor, but only with Doc Loveless' assistance. He wondered if he should go looking for the absent doctor or just stay in bed.

Outside the bedroom, a sudden creaking noise caught his ear, then the sound of soft footsteps treading over floorboards. Doc Loveless had left Badcock's bedroom door cracked slightly open, so he could see there was no light coming from the hallway.

"Doc? I mean, Mortimer?" Badcock called out from his seat on the bed, his voice growing louder as if to insulate himself from any danger. "Are you there?"

A light blinked on from somewhere in the hall but there came no reply, only the groan of a door opening. Badcock winced as he pulled himself to the edge of the bed, letting his legs lay limply over the side of the mattress. He then stood with some effort, the wound in his gut reminding him he might not get very far from where he had lain.

Walking stiffly to the door, Badcock grasped its knob and steadied himself, eventually stepping out into the dark hallway. The light he had seen was coming from another room, one at the hall's opposite end. The door to the room was ajar, as if beckoning him to enter.

Slowly, he reached the door's threshold and peered in. A bearded man in black suit sat at a writing desk, the light emanating from a gas lamp at its corner. His expression was pained, and he seemed engrossed in thought as he wrote fixedly with a quilled ink pen.

Badcock then recognized the man: it was his first business partner, Arthur Comstock. He had swindled Arthur of much of their shared funds and then left town, leaving him to likely bankruptcy. Soon after, Badcock had formulated his Tonic Bitters, using money he had cheated from the man. Badcock never knew what became of him.

Comstock put down his pen and wept softly, his face cradled in the palms of his hands. He opened the opened the drawer of the desk and took out a small pistol. Fatigued and defeated, he stared at the gun for a moment and then stood, fading into the shadows as the room went black.

Leaning on the frame of the door, Badcock turned as he heard a rope being hoisted from somewhere in the house, supporting wood creaking in response. He left the room and stood at the top of the floor's stairs; the figure of a man knelt at the stairs' bottom, a soft white glow surrounding him in the darkness.

Straining, Badcock kept a hand pressed against the walls of the staircase as he descended onto the floor below. The kneeling man was Atsa, his Indian guide in the territories, who he had betrayed for a bounty and then fled. Atsa's hands were tied behind his back, his long hair draped across his face.

Atsa staggered as he was yanked to his feet some force, then ascending nearby gallows steps, an empty noose waiting for him. The white glow illuminating the scene dimmed and went dark as the rope was placed around Atsa's neck, a tear running down his cheek.

Feeling ill, Badcock wiped beads of sweat from his forehead. A sickening dread washed over him as he grabbed the stairs' railing, weak and frightened. Where was he really? Was all this a nightmare, brought on by some infection-induced fever?

A light came on in the house's kitchen, not far from the stairs. Badcock heard someone rummaging through cabinets and a child quietly weeping, her terrible sorrow palpable from even where he took his short reprieve.

Pushing himself forward, Badcock stopped in the doorway of the kitchen. A haggard woman was desperately searching the place, as if looking for something to eat, but finding only bare cupboards. A small girl wearing a tattered dress sat on the floor, crying, her face hollow and emaciated.

It was his wife, Patience, and his young daughter, Charity. After *The Medicine Show* began to make profits, he had decided to abandon them, no longer wanting to provide for a family while on the road for so many months at a time. Patience had no way of supporting herself and Charity, so they would have fallen into poverty and eventually could have starved.

The kitchen darkened, leaving only Doc Loveless waiting at the end of the hall, his expressionless face revealed by light spilling out from the adjoining dining room.

"Doc, what's going on here?" Badcock said, his voice quiet, almost timid now. "Why am I seeing these things?"

"These scenes are the legacy of your life, Benjamin," Doc Loveless replied as an unsettling silence descended over them. "This is what you have left behind in the world past."

"World past?" Badcock almost fell into shock as he heard this. "Am I dead, Doc? But shouldn't I be in Heaven then?"

"Why would you be, Benjamin?" Doc Loveless seemed almost amused, his lips slowly curling into a sinister smile.

"Because my business is helping people, Doc," Badcock interjected, rising hysteria in his tone. "It's been my life's work. I sell hope to the hopeless and dreams to the dreamless. People need what I give them. I'm the good Samaritan."

Saying nothing in reply, Doc Loveless instead gestured toward Badcock with an open hand before making a guiding motion toward the dining room. "Come, you're the guest of honor at this gathering. There are still others you must meet tonight."

Doc Loveless slipped out of view as he entered the dining room. Badcock clutched the walls of the hallway with each step, holding himself up until he reached the dining room's doorway. Guests were gathered around a long table, china plates covered by domed silver cloches placed in front of each high-backed chair.

"Sit here," Doc Loveless bid Badcock, his hand indicating the unoccupied chair at the head of the dining table. "Dinner is served."

Instead of sitting, Badcock stood at the head of the table and looked out at the guests. Comstock was seated nearby, dark, treacly blood oozing from a gaping hole in his temple. Atsa sat across from him, his head tilted to one side, his swollen neck broken. Patience sat next to Atsa, her skin ashen and her eyes sunken, resembling a smiling skeleton.

Other guests were seated along the table, their faces showing signs of terrible maladies and terminal diseases, bought upon them with the aid of Badcock's "cure-all." The macabre guests watched Badcock intently, as if waiting for him to take his seat and begin the meal.

Badcock gazed down at his dinner setting on the table, a silver cloche covering his plate like the others. He cautiously removed the cloche and saw the head of a young girl, his daughter Charity's, its skin blotted by pestilence, with its eyes closed shut.

The head's eyelids snapped open as Badcock put the cloche next to the plate, its blackened tongue lolling out of its mouth, eyes rolling back into their sockets as the head produced a putrid gurgling noise. The dinner guests lifted the cloches from their plates, unveiling piles of bloody, cancerous tumors as the main course. Badcock then saw his gut had become a mass of squirming maggots, teeming, and festering in the place where he'd been shot.

Doc Loveless' eyes were pitch-black as he spoke, his voice hollow as if he was speaking from a distance void. "You've always served me, Benjamin Badcock, even without you being aware of it. But now, you will be the guest of honor for an endless night of ghoulish feasts, set before you on gilded platters, for all eternity."

Badcock screamed but there was no one to hear him. His place at the table would always be there and the spectral dinner guests would always be waiting for him, his banquet companions for all-time.

***

The man in the cattle hat leaned over a fatally wounded Badcock as he took his last dying breaths, the man's hands resting over his knees. Badcock's vision seemed to focus for a moment but then his head slumped to its side, his eyes closing for good with a faint gasp.

"See, I was right," the cattleman told his compadre, who was still mounted on horseback. "Two gunshots back from where I came; I knew he was in some trouble. But I think we're too late to help him."

The man on the horse asked in response, "Should we fetch the town marshal then? It's not like we can hide this wagon anywhere. Someone might come lookin'."

"No, I doubt it," the cattleman said, with a pleased smirk. "It's nighttime and no one heard the shots except us, probably. Let's just take what bills is in that paper box he stows in the wagon, and we'll be on our way. Make it look like a robbery, which it might have been anyway. Ain't no one gonna miss ol' Benjamin Badcock."

The Boneless King

The door to the cabin was unlocked, which Wes hadn't expected. He put the spare key back into his jeans pocket and pulled the cabin's peeling, weather-beaten entryway open, revealing a musty and neglected interior.

A single square room made up the entire space within, thick curtains pulled over the cabin's handful of grimy windows. Soft light spilled in through cracks in the window curtains, providing some illumination in the otherwise darkish place.

Dropping his canvas duffel bag onto the creaking floor, Wes strode to the room's center and hastily looked about, as if searching for something. There wasn't much furniture; only a four-legged wooden table, a solitary wood chair to go with it, and a battered couch resting in front of the empty stone fireplace.

He must have used the couch to sleep, Wes thought to himself, spying a rolled up wool blanket and two pillows for a makeshift bed. A thin layer of dust coated the silent room, likely proof that his missing uncle hadn't been back to this remote refuge of his any time in recent months.

But there was this: on the flat wood table sat a reel-to-reel tape recorder, a short stack of notebooks piled haphazardly nearby. The tape recorder was large and shaped like a box. Both audio reels contained a full spool of tape, enough to capture hours of dictation or other recordings. A small, hand-held microphone was attached to the recorder, its slim cord loose.

Wes sat on the table's well-worn chair, gingerly brushing away some grime with a hand before taking a seat. The tape recorder was plugged into a wall outlet, its power cable hanging over the table's edge. He turned the dial to 'PLAY' and listened as the reels began to slowly turn, a faint crackling noise soon quelled by the smooth, authoritative voice of the cabin's owner, Uncle Gordon:

I've returned from my year-long sojourn amongst the Munggua people. This formerly uncontacted tribe has endured as part of a fascinating, nearly pre-Neolithic culture found only on the western portion of the island. Their numbers are few, but the Munggua have held out in the unexplored jungles for many, many generations, perhaps since the earliest human habitation.

Within such an expansive area, the Munggua persisted in isolation until these past few years, making their ways unknown to outsiders. The Munggua even seemed to have believed they were the only people in existence, in a world all their own. My command of the native languages of the islands and the offering of gifts allowed me to live with these people, and to learn some of their most closely held secrets.

Turning the recorder's dial to 'STOP', Wes began sorting through the notebook pile on the table. The notebooks' pages were torn in places and sometimes heavily stained, as if Uncle Gordon had been writing while out in the field as he observed the practices of the *Munggua*. He randomly opened one of the notebooks and began to read a cursive, hand-written entry:

The necessary extract for the ritual is derived from several indigenous plants found in the jungles surrounding our village. Each inflorescent plant is poisonous in a large enough dose but when measured and then mixed, the effect is that of a neuroleptic instead.

The subject of the ritual must consume this substance from the shaman guide's bowl approximately one hour before its commencement. Otherwise, the shock would kill the subject before the final transformation is accomplished.

Wes closed the laboratory-style notebook and examined its cover. There was a date range jotted on a piece of adhesive tape near the cover's top but otherwise nothing indicating its contents.

There were ten notebooks in all, each detailing about a month of entries. Wes decided it would be easier to listen to the tape recordings first and then peruse the notebooks later. Perhaps his uncle had left some clue near the end of his tapes as to his current whereabouts. Wes' first year of medical school was over and he now had a several months' break to delve into this mystery.

The sun shone brightly as Wes stood on the cabin's threshold and scrutinized the limber pine woods around him, the midday light sharply contrasting the murky gloom found within the four walls of the cabin. He lit a cigarette and walked along the dirt trail leading up from the narrow combe where the cabin was nestled, the trail ending at a ridge above the valley.

Wes had hiked miles from the tertiary road where he had parked his rented truck to reach this spot. The forested valley was so secluded no other homes were anywhere near it, the cabin idling in complete solitude. The cabin's previous owners had apparently built the rustic abode as a hunting lodge of sorts.

Only he and Uncle Gordon knew about this place; Wes's father (and Uncle Gordon's brother) was unaware it even existed. Before leaving on this last sabbatical to the islands, his uncle had bought the small property for cash and had visited only once, living far away otherwise. With its deed, Uncle Gordon had included simple directions to the cabin, hidden away in a steel box kept in Wes' basement.

Why the secrecy? Uncle Gordon had told Wes he was the only one he could trust with the box and hoped that one day Wes would take over his studies, delving into the mysteries of the world's primitive peoples. He also seemed to hint that something important might be left for Wes at the cabin someday. What Uncle Gordon had intended to accomplish with this place was still unclear, its purpose elusive to his nephew. But he wanted to keep the secret.

Wes looked out over a panorama of hills and valleys as he stood atop the ridge, stark-white snow still cresting distant summits even in early summer. He finished his cigarette and tossed the butt onto the ground, taking in a deep breath of the cool mountain air. Wes thought back to when his uncle had first disappeared, near the end of Uncle Gordon's exploratory field leave from his research position, and how his father, Craig, did his best to help the police and Uncle Gordon's university with the open investigation.

"We've looked everywhere in this apartment," Craig said as he put another manila folder on the kitchen table, adding to the stack already there. "The police check earlier came up empty-handed, so we're wasting our time. I fear Gordon may really be the victim of foul play."

Craig seemed pained and then continued, after a sigh of tired exasperation. "My brother maintained fastidious records of his personal affairs, Wes. There's nothing Gordon might have kept here that Detective Becker could use in a missing persons case. We just have Gordon's financial papers, some legal documents, and..."

"What's this?" Wes interrupted, having opened the last folder taken from Uncle Gordon's at-home office by Craig. He then held up a medical form filled out with a typewriter. "This looks like a recent diagnosis from

Uncle Gordon's physician," Wes clarified, now seemingly intrigued. *"But I'm not sure what it's about."*

"Please let me see it," Craig requested, now standing over Wes, seated on a kitchen chair. His father quickly skimmed the form and then turned it over to read its back. *"Hmmm,"* Craig murmured, scratching his temple for a moment. *"I found this one folder under some loose papers at the bottom of a desk drawer. The police must've missed this."*

"It's a diagnosis for malignant glioma, a cancerous brain tumor," Craig finally announced, surprised. *"And this is from a neurologist, not Gordon's regular doctor. There's also a recommendation for treatment and surgery following the diagnosis."*

"Then Uncle Gordon could have been dying?" Wes asked urgently, realizing they may have found a genuine clue as to what had happened to his uncle.

"Yes, almost certainly," replied Craig as he read back over the form in his hands. *"Even with the tumor's removal, the survival rate for glioblastoma is low. Gordon had a few more years at most. I'll have to show this to Detective Becker tomorrow."*

Wes paused, uneasy, before asking another question. *"He may have taken his own life, instead of wasting away from cancer?"* Wes doubted this even as he said it, as Uncle Gordon was a stalwart fighter if there ever was one. Uncle Gordon would have never resignedly accepted his death from a disease. The man loved life more than anyone he had ever known.

"He could have, but where's the body? Something should have been found by now," Craig offered in response. *"The passenger manifest recorded he was on his return flight but there's no trace of Gordon after that. It was if he just vanished into thin air, without so much as a parting goodbye."*

"There's also no record here of a follow-up with the neurologist after his initial diagnosis," Wes indicated as he closed Uncle Gordon's medical records, putting the folder with its remaining papers on the stack. "He just left for his sabbatical in the months after without any further treatment, it seems. Odd that he wouldn't have tried to buy more time with surgery."

"True," Craig agreed, his voice becoming quiet; he seemed to be holding something back from Wes. "But, if he just wanted to die alone, why would he come back home? He didn't see any of us after his return. If he was planning an anonymous suicide, why not do it out on that faraway island, where no one would ever find the body?"

Wes rested at the table with the tape recorder, deciding not to smoke while in the cabin. He was worried cigarette smoke might somehow damage his uncle's tapes, and the air in the cabin was already quite noisome without tobacco fumes being added in.

Wes now knew Uncle Gordon had been very much alive after his plane trip home. He returned to this cabin, chronicling his stay among the *Munggua* for some archival purpose. But how did Uncle Gordon arrive here (Wes hadn't seen a vehicle left off the only accessible road here for many miles) and what happened after these tapes were recorded?

He pressed 'PLAY' again and the tape reels turned, Uncle Gordon's voice assuming a relaxed, narrative tone:

I have spent considerable time in other parts of this archipelago, but the magnificent vastness of the western island's lush tropical boscage still always takes my breath away. When viewed from the high hills not far from my host's village, the jungle canopy seems to have no end. The Munggua people live in a kind of untouched paradise, bountiful, where everything they could desire is within their reach. Even in post-contact, the Munggua remain fiercely protective of their privacy and native autonomy.

Their connection to the land is a profound one and informs the Munggua people's spiritual views. Reality to them is the flowering sago tree, the blue ocean, a turbulent, unchecked river, and an almost immeasurable, trackless mangrove swamp; this was the whole universe to the Munggua until strangers intruded on this way of life.

The Munggua believe that spirits inhabit all things, even their own bodily extremities. Certain spirits live in a man's fingers or nose, for example, and can cause mischief if offended or otherwise provoked. The Munggua also contend the spirits of their ancestors live on and watch over them, granting immense power which can be possessed through intricate ceremony and ritual sacrifice.

Herein lies my interest in these fervent, often-pitiless people: tribes I encountered on the island farther south, during previous expeditions, relayed tales of a folk who could metamorphize a man into a giant worm, the resultant worm form attaining nigh-immortality, even near godhood.

The name of this ritual of metamorphosis could be translated as "The Boneless King" as a worm is an invertebrate. It was this tribe's most sacred rite, and they considered it proof of their mastery over nature and the spiritual world.

The tribesmen who related this fable to me insisted it was true despite this fantastic claim. They then said the tribe who practiced this rite lived on the same island and were reputed to be flesh-eaters. The tribe was greatly feared and left to themselves, having head-hunted their neighbors to extinction in the distant past.

When the Munggua were first discovered by Westerners, the description of the Munggua's territory and the peoples' characteristics matched that of the "Boneless King" tales told to me by the island's local tribes. I knew, given my condition, that I must seek out the Munggua and learn the secret of their ritual. I had a rapport with the island people, and there was nothing left for me other than to wish for this chance to cheat death.

Uncle Gordon's narrative was cut short as Wes again put the recorder's dial to 'STOP'. He rummaged through his duffel bag where he had left it, near the cabin's tiny kitchenette area, finally removing a large brown envelope.

Wes slid from the envelope a black-and-white photograph, examining it closely. The photo was of Dr. Gordon Klingler, taken some years ago during his first journey to the islands.

Square-jawed and confident, Uncle Gordon stood at the center of a cluster of natives grasping spears. The men were grim-faced, as if they were enduring some unwanted intrusion but had been coaxed into posing for the picture anyway. Uncle Gordon appeared oblivious to the men's demeanor, instead smiling broadly at the camera in his jungle attire, his shirt sleeves rolled up to his forearms.

Putting the photo back, Wes stood and searched through the cabinets above the kitchenette's sink. He found two cans of corn beef hash, opening the cans with an opener left next to them. *Uncle Gordon didn't leave much food*, Wes thought, disappointed. *I'm glad I brought some of my own.*

One of the electric stove's burners glowed orange, a covered steel pot resting atop it. Wes drank thirstily from the sink faucet, hands cupped, as there were no drinking glasses, the rusted, iron-mineral taste of the well water disagreeable. He could faintly detect the whirring of a generator, the sound coming from somewhere below the cabin's floorboards.

He also left the generator running, a fire hazard, Wes considered, mildly concerned. *He must have, or I wouldn't have been able to run the tapes or use the stove without starting it back up. I wonder how much fuel I have left? I'll have to check later.*

Wes spooned the warmed hash onto a plate and went outside for lunch. He sat on some level rocks piled next to a thicket of trees and ate his simple meal in the afternoon sun. The old generator's whirring sound could be heard from outside as he sat close by to the cabin, the rumbling machine sometimes faltering with a sputter.

Wes pressed 'PLAY' as he sat at the table and then listened, Uncle Gordon's voice now vaguely anxious in parts as he spoke.

So, for months, I lived with the Munggua. They shared their rich oral tradition with me, celebrating and venerating their ancestors who they believe are still with them. As the Munggua and related island people have no written language, all their collective science, religion, history, and cosmology is passed on through storytelling, generation after generation.

I've transcribed much of their language in my notebooks, finding it very similar to many native dialects on the islands, but with some remarkable distinctions. I felt after some months' time I had gained these peoples' confidence. The Munggua seemed to see in me a kindred soul, despite my outsider's appearance.

Then, one night, the Munggua head man – his name is Kolokam – told me a new story, one I hadn't heard from any other village men before or subsequently. This story may be the tribe's oldest and, while not exactly a creation myth, implies the origin of the Munggua as a people.

In this story, a man called Gimi wandered alone for what seemed like an eternity to him, moving from place to place, until he came upon an uninhabited forest that would become the heart of the Munggua's tribal lands. Spent from his long travels, he fell to the ground under the sprawling jungle's tightly entwined cover, sinking into a deep and an interminable sleep.

Around Gimi's head, limbs, and bodily trunk, the tangled under-brush's porous soil started to claim him as he slumbered, restful and unaware. He was drawn down into the soupy, terrestrial detritus of the jungle floor, changing and reforming into a colossal, man-sized worm within this thin layer of earth.

More people came to this place and Gimi became their king, wor-shipped by them as a deity of the forest and the land. He protected his people and watched over them, elevating worthy elders to become "Bone-less Kings," a kind of sainthood among the Munggua. In the ground under their sacred place, these ancestors are ensconced, dormant in a prolonged estivation, but still heedful and aware.

This is the legend! This is why I had come to the Munggua, so I could learn this ritual of "The Boneless King," apparently real as I had hoped.

I questioned Kolokam, asking if he had ever seen an elder trans-formed into one of the revered guardian worms. Reluctant at first, he then said that he had and that it was an incredible sight to behold.

I asked if I could witness the ritual, if an elder had been chosen or soon would be. Kolokam was silent. He then slowly said one had been chosen, and that he would be the spirit guide to lead the transformation.

The Munggua had intended that I would leave them before the ritual, but I could view it if I so desired. The ritual would be held on a night of the new moon, in the thick of the jungle outside the village.

The night of the new moon came, and I was led to a secluded spot, perhaps a mile from where the Munggua maintained their settlement of thatched huts and flimsy rattan enclosures. A village man said they had kept this place in the jungle hidden from me until they felt I could be fully trusted. Now I was to see their most secretive and closely held rite take place.

I stood at the edge of a jungle clearing, perhaps with as many as a dozen other men within view. Upright wooden poles, carved with the

symbols of headhunting, adorned the clearing's edges. From the poles
hung shrunken human heads, the mouths of these unfortunates stitched
tightly shut.

Standing torches were interspersed among the headhunting poles,
their burning fires illuminating a bed of turned up soil at the clearing's
center. A naked man, very elderly and wizened, was guided by each arm,
and then lain down in the soil. The man appeared quite groggy and
benumbed, as if he had been thoroughly intoxicated beforehand.

The old man placed his arms over his chest and closed his eyes.
Kolokam appeared from the jungle's inky shadows, festooned in a
bird-feathered shaman's headdress and chalky-white face paint. A bone
ornament fashioned from the tusks of a wild boar protruded from his
nose, his expression contorted into an unnerving grin.

Kolokam was now as fearsome as could be imagined, letting out a
savage howl as he stood above the supine elder. His ceremonial stave was
held aloft, its raw wood twisted into the shape of a writhing flatworm.

The other men from the village drummed and sang and danced,
Kolokam chanting a refrain as the rest of the men shrieked and ululated.
They leapt from one side of the clearing to the other as they gyrated
frantically, a coarse sweat drenching their nearly bare bodies.

With their mouths hanging open, the men's eyes lolled back in their
heads, the spirits of this dark place having seized them and taking
possession of their souls. I felt as if I was peering through a window into
the very distant past, glimpsing a primeval spectacle that might have
been found at the beginning of man's antiquity.

As this enthralling display progressed, the elder suddenly began to
stir, his body at first showing only a tremor, but then falling into spastic
convulsions. A man was brought forth, a prisoner, and tied to one of the
headhunting poles. Kolokam would later tell me the man had murdered

his brother and that this was his punishment, to be consumed in an act of sacrificial cannibalism.

The elder's body bulged horrifically, his skin taking on a slick, jet black sheen. His limbs and torso swelled enormously, before collapsing into the shape of a monstrous dark brown worm, its pointed head long and snout-like.

The worm slithered toward the man lashed to the pole, the man trying to scream but his tongue had been cut out. His eyes protruded in terror as the worm engulfed his lower half, a glistening secretion beginning to dissolve the man's appendages.

I was both fascinated and repulsed by what was happening. The man soon went limp, the remainder of his carcass eventually disappearing into the smothering folds of the giant worm. Satiated, the worm burrowed into the soil where its human form had commenced the ritual, taking its place in the earth among the Munggua's forefathers.

The sun had almost set, the cabin dimly lit from the outside. Wes put the recorder's dial to 'STOP' when he finally noticed that evening had come. The jarring tale on Uncle Gordon's tapes made him forget where he was and what was around him.

A single lightbulb dangled from the cabin's panel ceiling, unshielded and unlit. Wes stood to pull the lightbulb's cord, bright light filling the cabin's middle interior, the table and chair where he had sat still in shadows.

Wes took a cigarette from a pack in his duffel bag and opened the cabin's front door. The air outside was cool, but this evening was warmer than the last. Soon, these mountains would bask in the summer heat, as they always did.

Lighting his cigarette, Wes inhaled its flavor, taking in a long draw through the cigarette's filter. He stared into the cabin from where he sat on a tree stump, the door propped open, light from the cabin ceiling's lightbulb spilling out into the surrounding night.

Wes thought back to when his father had dropped him off at home after searching Uncle Gordon's off-campus apartment. Father had said something odd, even disturbing, to Wes, possibly connected to the apprehension Wes had sensed from him when discussing Uncle Gordon's speculative murder or suicide.

Its wide bumper coming close to the sidewalk facing Wes' modest one-story bungalow, Craig parked his convertible, Wes sitting next to him in the passenger seat. Craig hoped Wes would be able to afford something better after medical school, even purchasing his first home if we wed upon graduation. But Wes was still single as far as he knew; he was tight-lipped about girls, as always.

"Well, here we are," Craig announced, watching his son push open the car door from the front seat. "I'll let you know what Detective Becker says after we speak on Monday."

Wes paused on the edge of his car seat and turned to look at this father. "Do you really think your brother would take his own life?" Wes asked emphatically, raising his voice as he did. "That would be so unlike Uncle Gordon. I can't believe he'd ever do it."

"Neither do I, really," Craig replied, looking away from Wes out onto the empty street, his expression preoccupied. "That's why I first suggested he was murdered instead. Years ago, Gordon confided something to me that I still think about."

"Like he was going to disappear someday, something like that?" Wes tensed, silently pleading that his father not to share even some worse.

"No," Craig answered. "He said that he was going to find a way to live forever, discover the secret of eternal life. Really. Gordon was entirely serious. He said this after his maiden voyage to the islands, quite a few

years ago. Seems very strange now, especially after his disappearance. I don't know what to make of it."

Closing the cabin door behind him, Wes sat on the table's chair and pressed 'PLAY', Uncle Gordon resuming his account of the *Munggua* and their customs.

There had been small signs of my growing weakness while on the island. Dizziness, followed by some nausea, and almost vomiting once or twice. I hadn't let Kolokam or the rest of the Munggua know that I was dying. If I had, they likely would have never allowed me to participate in the ritual, even as a trusted observer. My reasons for wanting to see the rite of "The Boneless King" would have been all too transparent then.

In bits and pieces, Kolokam revealed to me what is in the neuroleptic extract used in the ritual and thus I've recorded this information in my field notes. Interestingly, Kolokam stated all that's necessary for the transformation is the botanical extract and soil of the sacred grove, so infused with mystical potence is the earth there from millennia of ancestor worms resting under the dirt. The ritual chanting and cavorting are entirely for show, done to reaffirm the Munggua's religious traditions.

And a sacrifice. The sacrifice of a prisoner is effective, but the success of the ritual is almost guaranteed if a close family member is used in a prisoner's place. That the chosen relation comes to the place of sacrifice voluntarily is an absolute requirement.

The worm form can be achieved with the first two components of the ritual, but the new worm can only become forever undying with the sacrifice of a human life. A life for a life eternal.

I plan on digging in the sacred grove late in the night while the village sleeps, obtaining enough soil to...

Without warning, the light went out in the cabin and the tape recording stopped, as if the power had been abruptly cut off. Surprised, Wes stumbled from his seat and groped his way to his duffel bag, finding the camping flashlight he had brought for the trip. He flipped the flashlight's top switch on, and a wide beam shone onto the cabin floor, allowing him to see again.

I need to find the trapdoor for the cellar, it's got to be near a corner somewhere, Wes reasoned, probing around the room with his light source. *The generator's down there. Maybe it ran out of fuel finally.*

There was a dusty floor mat in a corner past the couch where Uncle Gordon set up his improvised bed. Wes turned over the mat with a foot, exposing a trapdoor with a handle. The hatch didn't seem locked.

Resting the flashlight on top of the tarp mat's turned-up leaf, Wes grabbed at the hatch's iron ring and pulled, opening the trapdoor into a set of short wooden stairs. Flashlight in hand, Wes crept down the steps into the darkness below.

The earthen cellar smelled of wet soil and gasoline, its underground atmosphere likely as stale as the cabin's air when he had arrived this morning. Crouching slightly beneath the low ceiling, Wes shined his flashlight along the walls of the cellar, spying the idle generator near its back. He began to step forward, in search of any fuel canisters he might use.

The ground beneath him was spongy as he approached, gleaming under the beam of his flashlight, the cellar's soil seemingly saturated with a fine coating of slime. His foot then sank, involuntarily caught on something.

A glinting, pointed tail whipped from the moistened dirt, wrapping itself around Wes's legs, and contorting itself around his waist and belly. He gasped in panic, falling back only to be enveloped by the humongous worm's fleshy interior lobes, digestive fluids dousing him.

One of Wes's arms was pulled into the worm's spiraling folds, their corrosive mucus burning his skin. Wes cried out and feebly struggled, his remaining arm quickly consumed and then finally his head, over-whelmed by the turning and undulating of the worm's massive body.

The invertebrate worm form of Uncle Gordon lay in the hallowed soil of the *Munggua*, having reached its primordial deification. It once again submerged itself into the floor of the earthen cellar, lying in wait for the warmer days ahead.

A Hunger So...

I am the sole survivor of a shipwreck, tossed into the ocean but saved by the whim of fate. The captain of our ship, may God rest his soul, failed to see the terrible storm that fell upon us until it was too late. That I was washed overboard and clung to some debris while others drowned, is entirely a matter of Providence and can only be explained by the Divine Will of Our Lord.

After that terrible night, I lay on a deserted beach, having found land as the ocean tides brought me in. I woke to the morning sun, having drifted into unconsciousness soon after washing ashore under cover of darkness. The white sands reflected brightly under my feet, the cloudless sky a hue of azure blue, palms trees swaying in the breeze not so far away from where I walked. What seemed like veritable paradise would only become a special Hell as I'll soon relate.

I walked among the detritus left from our former ship, *The Ascension*, picking through the broken wood and torn sailcloth, searching for anything I could use to survive. I found a broken mast, still intact enough to be of service. I dragged it back to the beach and began to construct a shelter against some rocks. I hadn't considered venturing farther into the island until I was more certain of any dangers which may be present.

The beams of the early midday sun became quite strong, yet the air was still cool due to the ocean breeze. I worked feverishly, not wanting to be caught unawares when the sun rose even higher. I was thankful for its brightness, for it allowed me to clearly see what I was doing.

I fashioned the mast into a sturdy frame for my makeshift shelter and then gathered ferns from farther away from the beach to form an improvised roof. Working with only what materials were at hand, my work was quick and efficient; absolute desperation driving me to complete this task as fast as possible. After several hours of labor, my shelter was complete; collapsing in its shade I surveyed my efforts: I had done well, better than anticipated.

I looked around at this new landscape – taking in all that surrounded me: deep blue water dotted with white foam crashing against rocks; lush green trees adorned with seagulls flitting between them... when suddenly something else caught my eye – a rat scurrying along sand staring at me with beady eyes!

The small black rodent seemed almost as if it watching me... Feeling uneasy yet curious about this strange creature, I continued exploring while ensuring always keeping an eye out for any movement from it; noticing often that it would stop – just long enough – to stare at me again before continuing on its way... Was there something it wanted from me? How could that be? It was only a rat.

I eventually decided to ignore this mysterious rat in order find food and fresh, potable water. Searching along the shoreline proved fruitless until discovering some sea grass which provided only meager sustenance before moving on.

The constructed shelter I had built was better suited for survival, not comfort. Weary days spent scavenging for food as well as the work of building led eventually to exploration of a network of dank caves, some distance from the white sands of the island's beaches.

Whereupon I entered these caves, I heard many strange sounds emanating from the darkness within. Peering far in the dark, I spied a black rat scurrying swiftly past, seemingly driven as if on a mission, more important than anything else to this creature.

For a moment, I felt an almost supernatural connection to the black furry thing, like an understanding of one another, though soon after I shook off these notions as mere imagination, a fanciful moment brought on by exposure to the strong sun.

Exploring farther into the caves' chambers revealed peculiar symbols painted upon the rocky walls, inspiring a kind of religious feeling in me despite my better judgement. My initial admiration gave way to an overwhelming dreadful presence, as if dark magic came forth from the black rocks piled near the far end of the caves. I was badly shaken, but continued on, suppressing an urge to flee in terror.

Upon touching the cold stone surface, I noticed these glowing symbols light up brightly, nearly blinding me with their brilliance. To witness these glyphs, giving the appearance of shifting and moving, almost pulsing with naked energy...I was strangely fascinating. The symbols' white light coursed throughout my body like a living thing, just as I was about to step away from them, out of harm's way.

Within a moment I knew why I was brought here: the rocks' ultimate purpose came to me, despite previously having no idea what the symbols or their relative placement meant. My eyes met the beady eyes of a rat, standing nearby on a low rock shelf in the cave.

Believing I must have been the one to bring the rate here, I feared the rat was part of a larger entity, a full rat's nest of its hungry fellows. What else might I discover here on this island, secrets held here for so long.

The rats may be the key to uncovering the mystery surrounding black rocks' origin within these caves. Both were of a jet-black hue and there was an odd, seemingly supernatural connection between the stones and the rats, enhanced by the strange symbols painted here. Who had painted them, and why so deep within the caves?

Without warning, an incredible vision appeared before me, out of thin air. It was a strange creature that seemed like a huge rat, but even larger, close to the size of a fierce dog; unlike anything I had ever seen before in my years on this Earth. I felt as if I was trapped in some sort of stasis, imprisoned within a dark void offering no escape. I could feel the creature's pain and despair, and I now knew that it needed my help.

I turned to the rat-thing and spoke to it, my not quite trembling voice filled with urgency. "What are you, creature?" I asked. "What must I do to help you? Please, tell me!"

The rat-thing simply stared at me, as if waiting for me to comprehend. I knew then that I was on my own, and that I alone must discover the secrets of the chamber and free the creature from its prison in the void. I had no other choice.

Determined, I began to study the symbols, trying to decipher their arcane meaning. I spent hours poring over the walls, tracing the intricate, swirling patterns with my fingertips. As I studied these glyphs, the symbols seemed to come alive, glowing, and again seeming to shift in response to my careful touch.

Days passed as I worked tirelessly, surviving on nothing but tepid water from a pool outside the caves and some fruits hanging from the ground-dwelling, flowering palm plants which grew everywhere on the island. More rats came, scurrying about the chamber as I toiled. My mind was consumed by the task at hand, and I barely slept, driven by an unrelenting need to uncover the secrets of the Black Rock and its symbols.

Finally, after what felt to me like an eternity, I deciphered the symbols of power. They were a map—a guide to a place beyond this world:

a realm of pure energy and light where the trapped creature could be freed and enter our world, at last.

Without hesitation, I set out on my journey following the map through a maze of tunnels and caverns deep beneath the Earth. The journey was treacherous; at times I feared I would never make it—but still pressed on driven by a fierce determination to save this creature, the rat-thing.

After another eternity of walking—I arrived at the Gateway to an otherworldly realm! I was finally here. But was it all an illusion? It was. I was back to where I began my journey into the caves, alone on this island prison.

I had been trapped on this island for probably weeks now. I desperately wanted a way to escape. I would often scavenge the beach for food and then scour the vast jungle interior in the hopes of finding some sign of civilization, anything really. I really had no other hope than to fervently wish, however remote my chances.

One fateful day, while exploring deep within the treacherous jungle, I heard a strange noise coming from behind one of the palm trees, surrounding by lush copses of fern plants. I cautiously stepped closer and peered around the palm tree only to see a teeming group of black rats - but not like any I had ever seen before, especially in their manners. They were much bigger than normal rats, but they also seemed to be twittering amongst each other, as if in conversation. Impossible, I know, but that's what it seemed to me.

I stood on my spot near the palm tree frozen in shock, watching the rats conversing among themselves, using high-pitched language I couldn't understand or decipher. Suddenly, one of them turned and noticed me standing there. The rat let out a loud screech that sent chills down my spine, as if commanding the others. I quickly ran back to my makeshift campsite, hoping that I wasn't being followed through the jungle.

When night fell, however, the rats began closing in on my camp on the beach. I heard their soft, padded footsteps getting closer and closer until they were right outside my torn cloth tent, made from the sails of our broken ship. I realized then that these rats weren't just intelligent - they wanted to eat me! Rats desire the flesh of men, always and in all places, with a lust that can't be a described. A hunger so...

I desperately tried to fight them off, but the pulsating mass of black fur and sharp teeth eventually swarmed over me and overpowered me, taking me down to the sands of the beach. I screamed and fell into unconsciousness, sure I was to be devoured by these bestial creatures, driven only by the basest of primal urges.

The next morning, the sun shone on my face, bloody and swollen. I awoke deep within the rat's subterranean den, finding himself surrounded by the same group of rats I had seen before, from what I could gather. I felt as if I could now understand what they were saying as they twittered, for their high-pitched language was one of gnawing hunger and the rank desire for my flesh, however degraded it was!

Horrified, I desperately pleaded for my freedom, but the rats only seemed laughed at me, the shrill twittering becoming nearly deafening, a hundred minute throats in chorus with one another. The leader of the pack then spoke out in a tiny voice filled with malice: "We have been waiting for you, human," it said, standing on its hind legs, its paws before it. "Welcome to our island retreat - your new home, forever."

I screamed in terror. I was dragged away again, this time into the darkness, by the snarling pack of black rats, I feared never to be seen or heard from again. I was shipwrecked on a desert island, these bizarre, intelligent rats who seemed to be a new species, my masters, one unknown to mankind before now.

But then I awoke. This was yet another nightmare, my mind consumed by an intense fever, my body drenched in cold sweat. Was it the water I had drank from the pools, perhaps polluted? Was it one of the ripening fruits I had eaten, perhaps poisoned? I wasn't sure.

I was so relieved when I finally made it back to the beach with the broken mast. It had taken me hours of careful, meticulous work to secure and drag to the shoreline, but I wasn't about to give up no matter how hard my muscles ached or how exhausted I felt.

Finally, as the sun began its ascent in the sky, I started piecing together my makeshift shelter, which had fallen into despair during my period of unconsciousness. How long had I been unaware? I don't know.

I worked quickly, driven by fear that something might come for me while I was still vulnerable and exposed on this lonely island. As if a warning from some otherworldly being, an eerie chittering sounded around me--it seemed like every creature on this forsaken place knew of my presence. Rats?

Suddenly, a black rat scurried out from under a pile of debris not far away from where I stood. Its eyes were huge and menacingly dark as they stared at me hungrily--the rat wanted nothing more than to sink its sharp teeth into my flesh!

With one last burst of energy fueled by sheer terror and adrenaline, I threw myself onto the ground beneath my shelter just in time before two more rats emerged from their hiding places nearby. The rats joined their friend in trying desperately to get into what appeared to be a safe haven for them all....

The rats circled me like sharks in water as they closed in on their prey; there seemed to be no escape from certain death. Then suddenly something miraculous happened—a flock of seagulls flew overhead and scared away the rodents before they could do any harm! I was lucky, in more ways than just one.

It appeared fate had given me a second chance at life after all! Grateful beyond words for being saved by such an unlikely intervention, I thanked God above for His Mercy and protection from harm. The rats had fled, back into the jungle from whence they came.

I had nothing but the clothes on my back and a broken mast as I looked around at what was left of the wrecked ship. It felt like an age since I'd been thrown overboard, so far from land that there seemed little chance of survival. But here I was, standing on the beach with a plan to save myself, however remote.

I used all my strength to drag the mast onto the sand and began to build a shelter from it, also using some branches from nearby palm trees. As I worked feverishly, dreading that if I took too long in finishing then nightfall would arrive before me, foraging rats started appearing on the island, among the underbrush.

Their eyes gleamed hungrily at me as they scurried about looking for food - unfortunately for them it seemed that their meal might be me! I had to escape.

The thought made me work faster until finally my simple shelter was complete just in time for sundown, the rays of the tropical sun disappearing over the horizon.

Panting with exhaustion and fear, I crawled inside it just moments before darkness descended upon us both – thankfully only one of us would make it through this night alive...

I had no idea how long I'd been on the island, but all I knew was that it felt like an eternity since *The Ascension* had gone down into the churning ocean during a storm. I walked slowly and cautiously through the dense jungle at night, desperately searching for signs of life.

Suddenly, I heard a noise coming from behind a large rock. My heart started beating faster as I crept closer to investigate, aware I could be in danger.

As I rounded the corner of the rock, I was horrified by what I saw: a horde of flesh-hungry black rats scurrying around the grassy space, squealing, and twittering. I backed away slowly, but it was too late - they had already noticed me. The rats seemed highly intelligent; they were communicating with each other and planning their attack, as if they were soldiers in a murine army. Where was their general?

I tried to run, but the rats were too quick - they had me surrounded before I could make my escape. I screamed for help that didn't exist as the rats slowly advanced on me, their razor-sharp teeth glinting in the moonlight.

I was certain that this would be my end and closed my eyes, waiting for the inevitable. But then, a miracle happened - a loud noise echoed through the jungle, scaring away the rats. I opened his eyes to see that I had been saved by a flock of seagulls who had frightened off the rodents. I was saved, for now.

I sighed in relief as I watched the rats flee into the darkness. I thanked my lucky stars that I had been saved, but I knew that the island was still no place for a man - not with those flesh-hungry rodents lurking in the shadows. I vowed to never stay on an island again and dreamed of returning home, praying for a second chance at life. But how would I make my escape? I was alone, surrounded by the boundless ocean.

I would build a raft from the palm trees and push it out to sea. That I would find dry land or that a passing ship would rescue me was my only hope. The rats would get me if I didn't hatch and execute this mad, bold plan to leave the island.

The Empress

Miranda sat on the floor of the dimly lit bathroom, peering down into a silver hand mirror. She turned her head to view her profile, the palish light from a solitary candle casting foreboding shadows over her face. Miranda had never liked her own face very much; she wished instead that she resembled her mother or perhaps her   sister,   Samantha,   blonde   and

g   l   o   w   -

ing.

Miranda would turn eighteen next week and, the month after, graduate from high school. She frowned as black strands fell across her eyes and brushed them aside, her hair framing her oval face in a neatly cut veil. Miranda had been sitting on the bathroom floor almost since her classmate, Veronica, had left, gazing into the mirror she had found in her mother's dresser drawer.

"Really, just stare into the mirror," Veronica had told her, "and ask for 'Jane.' Wait a bit, and then say something like 'Jane, will I ever get married?' or 'Jane, will I ever fall in love?'" Veronica paused for a moment and raised an eyebrow, a faint smile playing on her lips. "Jane might even show you her frightening face after answering and ask, 'Do you think I'm pretty?' Don't hesitate. You'd better say 'yes' right away!"

Miranda leaned forward at the kitchen table and rested her arms across her textbook. "You're just trying to scare me," she said in an annoyed voice. "I don't believe a word of it."

Veronica held up both hands in protest and smiled again, this time breaking out into a broad grin. "My sister—you know, Melissa?—she swears it's all true. A friend of a friend told her the story. Says it happened at the friend of a friend's cousin's school all those years back. But why don't you just find out for yourself?"

Standing up from her seat at the table, Veronica looked around the kitchen. "I would use a hand mirror as you can just drop it if she shows you her ugly mug. Seeing Creepy Jane's face in the bathroom mirror would be way too scary."

Miranda had expected a quiet evening at home preparing for final exams but Veronica quickly began teasing her about boys. Dateless throughout high school, Miranda was set to begin college without ever having had a boyfriend. The two girls had known each other since middle school and their friendship was close, but there had always been a rivalry between them.

"School has just always been my priority." Miranda looked away defensively. "Besides, boys don't seem to like girls who are smarter than they are. And I'll remind you, you're the one struggling in pre-calc—even if you do have Tony."

Veronica said nothing, only smirking from the other end of the table.

"Whatever. Let's get this done," Miranda said brusquely. "Mom and Samantha are coming home from the recital in a couple of hours." Opening her pre-calculus textbook and reaching for her notes, she looked down at the papers with renewed focus.

"Have you ever heard of Creepy Jane?"

That was how it had all begun. Veronica had slumped in her chair, a physical expression of her disinterest in solving more math problems, her thin lips curved into a mischievous grin.

"Isn't that your aunt?" Miranda said without looking up from her textbook.

"No, silly, Creepy Jane is what they call an 'urban legend.' A story about some tragedy or some monster that no one can prove is real, but the story gets spread around anyway. But this one is real, believe me."

Miranda stopped leafing through her notes and glared at Veronica. "Do you want to pass this class or not?"

Veronica sat up in her chair and her smile vanished. "Okay, just let me tell you this one story and then we can get back to work. Is it a deal?"

Intrigued despite her better judgment, Miranda nodded silently. Veronica was a middling student, but she was quite creative and imaginative when the occasion presented itself.

Veronica looked away from the kitchen table, wrinkling her brow and pursing her lips. When she turned to face Miranda again, her eyes were piercing, holding a curious expression of genuine fear.

"Jane was a high school girl who lived many years ago—in the 1960s or something—and was mercilessly bullied by her classmates. She was awkward, with clunky glasses and braces on her teeth; homely to begin with but with looks made worse by having no style and no social skills.

"Jane had always been an outcast, but her abuse by the others reached a whole new level when she started high school. A group of mean girls a few grades ahead gave her the nickname 'Creepy Jane' and it stuck.

"One day, after being humiliated by these girls in front of the morning assembly, she went into the girls' restroom and ate rat poison—the entire box—which she had taken from the janitor's closet. A teacher found her dead in one of the stalls after she didn't show up for her afternoon class, her face horribly twisted and discolored.

"Soon after, those six girls who had bullied her the worst started to die or disappear one by one. Rumor had it that Creepy Jane's face would appear in their bathroom mirrors before each of them died or vanished, wearing that dreadful death mask the French teacher had found etched on her face. Within just months, all of the girls were either dead or gone. Never to be found."

Miranda swallowed despite herself, fighting off a tingling feeling creeping up her spine.

"The legend says that if a girl sits in a dark bathroom with a lit candle, stares into a mirror, and asks for Jane, she might just receive a reply from the spirit world," Veronica said. "Jane might be friendly, or she might not. That's the risk you take to know the future!"

Miranda stared at Veronica incredulously, the fingers of her right hand searching for a pencil.

Veronica was quiet for a moment, and then became insistent. "Really, just stare into the mirror and ask for Jane. Wait a bit, and then . . ."

Veronica waved as she opened her car door and then took a seat behind the wheel. Miranda stood on the porch steps, considering how much time she had left before Mom and Samantha walked in through the front door. Maybe an hour? More than enough time to find a mirror she could use to summon Creepy Jane. She scoffed to herself at the idea.

Miranda sat down on the living room couch and reached for the remote control, turning on the television. She started to watch a reality dating show, the light from the television set flickering in the otherwise dark room.

The young female contestant was asking each of the handsome, eligible bachelors a question about themselves. The last question the woman asked before the commercial break was "Have you ever been in love?"

Miranda fidgeted uncomfortably and turned to look over her shoulder at the entrance to the hallway, which ended at the first-floor bathroom's door. Shutting off the television, Miranda walked up the stairs to her mother's bedroom in the now-silent house. The spacious room was still cluttered with boxes from their recent move following her parents' divorce late last year.

Mom had taken some things she had found in their new home's attic and kept them here, somewhere in her room. Miranda remembered watching from the hallway outside as her mom put an ornate hand mirror into the dresser drawer.

Buried under layers of clothes in the bottom drawer, the mirror was wrapped in a white linen cloth. Miranda took the looking glass by its handle and held it in front of her. It was surprisingly weighty.

The mirror was made of sterling silver and appeared Victorian in origin. It was probably over a century old, with floral flourishes and a beveled edge. *Why would Mom have hidden the mirror here instead of just placing it on top of the dresser?* Miranda asked herself, perplexed.

Near the center of the mirror's back side was the image of a smiling young lady, her long, flowing hair framed by a wreath of flowers. Miranda decided such an antique object would be perfect for a séance with the spirit world—what better than the possession of some English lass now long dead?

Returning downstairs, Miranda took a candle in a small jar and a box of matches from the kitchen cupboard. She lit the candle on the bathroom sink countertop and then sat on a shaggy bathmat, squinting in the poor light at the mirror's round surface.

This is crazy! Miranda thought, nearly standing to put the mirror away in a drawer. Instead, her eyes searched the bathroom, glancing at the nylon shower curtain and the colorful bath towels hanging on the rack nearby. She took a deep breath and looked into the mirror once again.

"Jane?" Miranda said quietly, a nervous tremble in her voice.

Nothing.

"Jane?" Miranda said a second time, almost whispering. "Jane, will I meet my future husband at school?"

Silence.

The candle's flame flickered in its jar and the room grew darker for the briefest moment. Miranda's head turned quickly—she thought she'd heard a girl's laughter and then a soft sigh, but the sound had faded instantly.

A shape began to form within the mirror's frame. Miranda swallowed as she leaned forward, trying to make out its details. It was a person's face, but its features were too indistinct to tell who it might be. Slowly, the face of a girl came into hazy focus, smiling . . .

Sharon shook, her tears unending, her face buried in the wet palms of her hands. She heaved and gasped on the front steps of her home, her anguish palpable. A young police officer stood nearby, waiting for her to stop crying, if only for a moment.

"Here, Mrs. Ortiz, please take two of these with water," the officer said calmly, proffering two tablets in a packet and a foam cup. "Swallow them and then try to breathe normally, through your nose instead of your mouth. You may have a panic attack if you don't."

"I can't . . . I need to just sit here," Sharon managed, looking up at the officer through red, swollen eyes. "I can't go back inside the house!"

The officer nodded, her face a mask of understanding. "You won't need to, Mrs. Ortiz. A squad car will bring you and your daughter to the police station. A detective can take both of your statements there."

Sharon tore open the small paper package and tossed the tablets into her mouth before drinking. Several police cruisers were parked on the neighborhood street, their rolling lights flashing over the exterior of the house in the nighttime darkness. An ambulance had pulled up in the driveway and two paramedics were wheeling a covered gurney toward it.

Sharon's mind swam. She dropped the empty cup on the wooden step, which was the only thing she could really feel at this moment. In body and in soul, Sharon was numb everywhere; her eldest daughter, her beloved Miranda, was gone—strangled to death on the bathroom floor of their home.

The police officer helped Sharon to her feet and eased her aside as the paramedics passed them, the gurney rattling behind. They lifted it up the steps and disappeared into the house. Sharon heard a police body bag being zipped open and almost retched.

She turned her back on the scene and walked toward her daughter, Samantha. Samantha was speaking to a second police officer under the front lawn's tall, sheltering oak tree, who was hastily jotting notes down on a pad.

"Like I said, the front door and the bathroom door were both locked when we came home. Officer Williams and his partner had to force the bathroom door open with some tools after we called 911. That's when we found Miranda." Dried tears stained Samantha's face, but she had held her composure throughout the emergency call and even during the discovery of Miranda's body. Miranda's throat had been crushed as if with great force—Sharon imagined her daughter being strangled by some large and powerful escaped lunatic.

The officer put away his notepad and studied Samantha for a moment, wondering whether there might be more to this incident than the young girl was telling him. "There are no signs of forced entry either," he said, offering Samantha another tissue from his shirt pocket. "Officer Williams searched both floors of the house, and the windows and doors are secure. You confirmed too that nothing appears to have been stolen."

The police officer briefly looked away to scan the house, and then met Samantha's gaze. "The only person who may have seen Miranda tonight other than you and your mother is Veronica Peters, her classmate at University High School. Is that right?"

Samantha saw her mother walking toward them. "That's right. Veronica and Miranda were supposed to study for finals tonight. Please call her parents and make sure Veronica made it back. I've got her number here somewhere..."

The paramedics wheeled Miranda's corpse out on the covered gurney and loaded it into the back of the waiting ambulance. Neither Sharon nor Samantha looked on as the paramedics did their work; both were still haunted by the nearly indescribable expression of horror on Miranda's face, her blood-saturated eyes staring up at the bathroom ceiling.

The police officer ushered Samantha and her mother back toward the house. Grim business indeed. He glanced again through the squad car's window at the clear evidence bag slung on the back seat. A strange antique mirror caught his eye, almost seeming to stare back at him.

***

"Yes, we've moved back in for now. No, I don't think we'll sell, especially if you say there's a chance a new lead might turn up. Thank you, Detective, I'll stop by the station some time for the mirror if you don't need to hold onto it any longer. It's a quite valuable heirloom—it belonged to the house's original owner. Thank you." Sharon hung up the phone and turned to Samantha.

"Your sister's case has been closed," she said quietly. "Detective Sherman says the department still has no solid leads. They're assuming it's a random killing at this point. The case is cold unless new evidence comes to light." She put a hand over her mouth and took a shaky breath as she searched Samantha's face for a reaction.

Samantha stood from her chair at the kitchen table and hugged her mother, the two embracing in silence for several long moments. Finally, Sharon gently pushed Samantha away and said in a reassuring voice, "We can keep hoping that something comes up. But we need to get on with our lives." Looking away with a pained expression, she added, "But your father won't be of any help to us. I haven't heard from him since the funeral."

Samantha sighed. "We don't need him. Dad's going to start a new family now that he's moved out of state. He'll forget about us, just you watch."

"Your father's wandering eye—and other body parts—are why we divorced to begin with," Sharon said, forcing a laugh.

Playing along, Samantha grinned. But the truth was that both she and her mother felt uneasy about moving back into the house. The police had spent days collecting forensic evidence, and a crime scene cleanup had been completed by a private company. It was, technically, all ready for them to move back in, but to Samantha it all felt too soon.

Neither she nor her mother was superstitious, but Miranda's death had been so violent... It was enough to threaten anyone's peace of mind. Detective Sherman had warned them that the killer was likely still out there and may even return. He'd ordered an increase in the number of neighborhood police patrols as a precaution.

The autopsy had found that only a hulking man with incredible physical strength could have caused Miranda's injuries. Yet, curiously, there were no marks or even fingerprints on Miranda's throat. The killer may have wrapped a towel around her neck before strangling her, but no towel with evidence of the crime was found and none were missing from the bathroom. And Miranda's face... Well, no one could forget such a frightful visage.

***

That Saturday, Samantha drove her mother's sedan to the local shopping mall to purchase some school supplies. Sharon's car now conspicuously displayed a sign stating "Student Driver," which was visible from both the front and rear of the vehicle.

Samantha parked near the movie theater and walked through a revolving glass door into the mall's lobby. Hurrying past the shops that lined the main thoroughfare, Samantha stepped onto the escalator. The office supply store was right at the top.

The woman behind the cash register smiled pleasantly at Samantha as she put notebooks and other supplies into a plastic bag. "Summer's almost over. Are you excited to be going back to school?"

"Sort of. I'll be glad to be out of the house," Samantha answered, looking past the woman to the shops on the opposite side of the mall's second floor. She spotted Miranda's old friend, Veronica, folding sweaters and shelving them on a display in the front window of a clothing store.

Samantha picked up her bag and hurried across the concourse, weaving through the shoppers passing her by. "I didn't know you worked here," Samantha said, stopping at the window display.

Veronica turned and seemed surprised. She put down the cotton sweater she was holding and managed a half-smile. "Samantha, hi. How are things coming along? I haven't seen you since Miranda's funeral back in April."

Samantha was immediately taken aback by how fatigued Veronica appeared; there were bluish-dark circles under her eyes and fine creases around her mouth. "Mom and I moved back into the house this week," she replied. "I'm getting ready for the school year. We're trying to get back to normal, but it's hard."

"You're not afraid to live there after what happened?" Veronica said, with legitimate concern. She then looked over her shoulder as if searching for a manager—or perhaps, Samantha thought suddenly, someone else—who might be watching them.

"We don't have much of a choice, really. Mom just bought the house, and we'd have to sell at a huge loss. Miranda's death was on the news for like a whole week." Samantha gave a deflated sigh. "Every real estate agent would tell their buyers about what happened. The house is a no sell."

Veronica nodded weakly. Samantha couldn't get over it—the girl had utterly changed since Miranda's burial service several months ago. Veronica seemed not only tired, but truly exhausted, almost entirely drained of her usual good humor and vitality. She seemed now a liminal figure, as if steadily fading away, from the daylight and into the shadows.

"I don't want to sound crazy, but don't you believe in ghosts?" Veronica's smile persisted, but Samantha could tell she was quite serious.

Samantha stiffened. "No, I don't. And neither does Mom. Living in a murder house is a bit spooky, but dead is dead."

Veronica's eyes suddenly darted left and right as Samantha uttered this last phrase.

"Mom keeps the first-floor bathroom shut tight, but only because we don't want to use it," Samantha continued. "It's too painful for us right now. Maybe someday we'll open it back up, but not any time soon."

"I believe in ghosts," Veronica said softly. "I do."

"Veronica, is something wrong? I mean, are you sick or something?"

"No, why would you say that?" Veronica forced a wider smile and hopped slightly—a feeble attempt to perk herself up.

"You just seem different from when I saw you last. Like you're not getting enough rest."

"Oh, I'm just a bit worried about starting college next month," Veronica said, waving a hand dismissively. "Excited and worried. Sleep has taken a back seat to getting ready for my first semester away from home." Veronica looked away again, as if afraid to say more.

"I have to get going," Samantha said slowly, backing away. "School is starting for me too. My junior year at Uni High." Samantha snickered nervously. "I bet you won't miss that place."

Veronica changed the subject instead of answering. "Do the police have any new leads or is it pretty much done?" She seemed hopeful now, more engaged than she had been for much of their conversation.

"It looks like it's done," Samantha answered. "Whoever did it needs to be caught, but the police have nothing to go on. They even took that funny mirror Mom kept in her room as evidence, but found no fingerprints other than Miranda's."

"You said a mirror? What kind of mirror?" Veronica instantly became animated, her deadened eyes widening.

"An old hand mirror. It's... some antique that came with the house," Samantha said as she furtively glanced at her wristwatch. "Our agent told us only one other family lived in the house between us and the original builders: a married couple with four boys. The family left everything in the attic alone, even though they knew some of the things stored there were probably collector's items."

Veronica fell into silence. A few customers passed by them as the girls conversed, but none interrupted.

"When we were studying that night, before I left, I told Miranda about Creepy Jane." Veronica now seemed on the verge of tears.

Samantha frowned. "Who or what is Creepy Jane?"

"I told Miranda it was an urban legend, but it was just a story I made up on the spot," Veronica said, sniffling as she wiped a closed eye with her fingers. "I wanted to scare her a bit, just for fun. But she may have tried what I told her to do."

"You told her to look into a mirror?"

"Not just that, but to call for Jane while gazing into a mirror in a dark bathroom. Don't use the bathroom mirror, I said—light a candle, and then call for Creepy Jane. Ask Jane if she'll find you a husband while staring into the mirror." Veronica managed a small smile as she recited the instructions. "It's nonsense, of course, but something might have gone wrong. I never told the police when they questioned me because I didn't think it was important."

"I doubt that mirror has anything to do with it," Samantha countered. "The bathroom door was locked from the inside—that's the part the police detective couldn't figure out. They don't know how the killer got in."

Veronica shivered and pulled at her button-down sweater. "I'd move out if I were you," she said in a hollow voice. "You shouldn't stay in that house. It's not safe for you and your mom."

Samantha was unshaken by this revelation about her sister's death. "The mirror is just an old mirror, Veronica," she offered. "Miranda probably wanted to store it away in the bathroom drawer when she was attacked... or whatever happened."

Veronica hugged Samantha tightly and said, "I'll see you at Christmas when I get back from school. Take care of yourself."

Bemused, Samantha walked toward the escalator and briefly wondered if she should examine that odd silver mirror once Mom retrieved it from the police station.

"Why would Veronica fill your head with a crazy story like that? I'm not surprised, though. I always thought that girl was a liar." Becca sat with Samantha and their friends at the picnic table, interjecting right after Samantha finished her tale. "Creepy Jane sounds about as real as Veronica's bustline," Becca declared, her manner as mocking as ever.

Lily and Ava snorted with laughter as Samantha shifted uncomfortably. Becca had called late in the afternoon and suggested she and the girls "hang out" at the park near Samantha's house that evening. School would start again in a few weeks, and everyone wanted to savor the last vestiges of warm summer weather before they had to once again spend all day sitting in a classroom.

"It's just... it's so strange. Why would Miranda have had Mom's hand mirror with her unless she really was trying to contact Creepy Jane? There's a lighted vanity mirror above the sink. If she were combing her hair or something, she would have used the bathroom mirror." Samantha looked around at her friends, genuinely worried that the circumstances of Miranda's death could be even more bizarre than anyone had previously imagined.

The small public park was mostly empty; only a few couples and cyclists passed by in the distance. Becca smiled and reached across the picnic table to touch Samantha's hand reassuringly. "Veronica may somehow be blaming herself for your sister's death. You said she looked wiped out, like she's not getting enough sleep. Maybe she's 'remembering' things that never really happened."

Samantha examined the youthful faces of the girls, all of whom she had known since childhood. *What do they think of me now?* Samantha considered. There had been an outpouring of sympathy from her classmates and neighbors following Miranda's murder, but there was, she knew, a limit to any grieving period. Samantha had been hesitant to share what she had been told by Veronica, but she'd needed to tell someone of her fears, her growing suspicion that something very peculiar had occurred that night.

"I have an idea. Let's break into the school and see if Creepy Jane shows up in the restroom mirror when we call for her. Then we'll know if Veronica is telling the truth or if it really is just an urban legend." Jumping up from her seat on the bench, Becca smiled at the other girls in the receding twilight. "It'll be some wicked fun before we're sent off into slavery again." She clapped her hands together with glee as she spoke.

"You're an idiot. We'll be caught and suspended before school even starts. Sit back down or go home." Ava shook her head, exasperated. "This 'Creepy Jane' is an urban legend; there's nothing to it," she said scornfully.

"I've climbed through one of the pool building windows before with Aaron Rogers," Becca said slyly. "We went swimming at night

and then escaped through the side door near the offices. That old janitor, Carl, is too careless to lock everything up, especially the windows."

Becca began to walk toward her waiting SUV and waved at her
friends to follow her. "I'm going, even if none of you are," she said over
her shoulder, passing the sand-covered playground near the picnic
tables. "If there's nothing to it then at least we'll get to go for a swim
in the pool."

Lily stood up and followed Becca without saying anything. She
had been observing their banter but had only become engaged when
Becca announced her plans for a midnight swim. Ava looked over at
Samantha, who glanced at her, smiled apologetically, and then stood
up to follow Becca. Rolling her eyes, Ava followed.

***

"Hold my flashlight, will you?" Becca said, thrusting it to Lily as
she crouched near the window. "I'll climb through." Becca dropped
her compact gym bag onto the grass in front of her before pulling
the frame of the large, partially open awning window outward, its
ill-maintained hinges creaking.

The crank window's stiff hinges held in place, allowing Becca to
squeeze under the frame and carefully drop down onto the pool
room's blue-tiled floor. Standing at the edge of the full-length swimming pool, Becca looked around and then motioned for Lily to throw
her gym bag through.

Becca bent over to pick up her bag and then walked behind the
diving board, pushing open the door to the girls' locker room. The

reflection of the dimmed ceiling lights on the water sent a kaleidoscope of rippling shapes spinning across the tiled walls of the pool room.

Lily turned to Ava and Samantha who were standing watch behind her and whispered, "Come on, Becca said to wait by the coach's office." The three girls walked around the length of the school natatorium and found the path to the building's side door. They then waited patiently in the dark for Becca to appear.

Soon, the metal door clicked and then slowly opened. Becca was standing in front of them in a one-piece swimsuit, beaming from ear to ear. "Get inside, someone might see you!" she breathed hurriedly. "I'm going to do some laps around the pool before we try our phone call to the dead."

Samantha closed the door behind them and followed the girls down an unlit hallway past several locked offices and into the pool room. Becca lowered herself into the chlorinated water, attempting not to make too much noise. She did a few laps and then swam in broad circles, drifting through the water on her back as she paddled with her arms.

Lily sat on one of the wooden benches placed against the walls and took off her sneakers and socks. She stripped down to her underwear and then stepped into the pool, dropping down into the water with an audible *plop* and vanishing beneath its surface. She bobbed up a moment later and grinned, pushing back her long, wet hair with her hands.

Ava and Samantha took seats on a wooden bench at the opposite side of the pool, watching Becca and Lily eagerly muck about. After a short while, Samantha glanced at Ava and the two of them stood and walked toward the girls' locker room.

Samantha purposely left the lights off as they entered to not risk attracting the attention of Carl the janitor. Becca had set down her gym bag on one of the benches dividing two rows of metal lockers; Samantha easily found the neon-colored bag even in the semi-dark. The locker room was deathly quiet, with only the distant sound of splashing breaking the silence.

"Becca said she put the candle and matches from the SUV's compartment in here," Samantha noted as she unzipped the bag's top and began to fish around inside. "Her dad insists she keep an 'emergency' candle with a box of matches in the SUV in case of a blizzard."

Ava laughed. "There hasn't been snow in the Central Valley in probably ten years."

"You're right. But she goes skiing with her family up in the mountains. You never know when a candle might come in handy."

Samantha unscrewed the circular lid and saw that three wicks were embedded in the candle's wax surface. She placed the open tin on the grooved rail running beneath the bench's wall-mounted mirror. Ava looked over her shoulder, catching Samantha's eyes in the mirror. "Sam," she said hastily. "The splashing's stopped."

Samantha listened. "They must be out of the pool. Go grab them so we can do this. The longer we stay, the more we're pushing our luck."

"But this is a real thrill, right?" Ava replied, her smirking face only faintly visible. "See you in a moment."

As Ava left, the locker room door creaked open and then closed with a thud. Samantha looked around in the dark, not truly afraid but beginning to feel a chill. The door to the locker room opened again.

"Ava?" she called.

No response, no footsteps—nothing but the sound of the door swinging shut.

There was a dark shape standing at the end of the lockers, watching her. Samantha squinted. "Yes, Ava, very funny. Come on, where are the others?"

The figure moved across the open space between the rows of lockers, disappearing behind them. Samantha swallowed. She rubbed her hands over her forearms and slowly stepped forward to peer around the edge.

Nothing was there. The chill in the air had become more pronounced.

Then, movement out of the corner of her eye. Samantha spun and caught a glimpse of the back of a girl's head, long tresses flowing as she disappeared through the now-open locker room door.

As the door swung closed, it was almost immediately pushed open from the outside. Ava, Lily, and Becca stepped into view, giggling amongst themselves. Samantha faced them and saw that Lily and Becca had wrapped towels around their midsections. Lily was grasping her clothes and the collars of her sneakers with both hands.

"Hey, let's get this done. Light that candle," Becca said, coming to a stop in front of the face-level rectangular mirror. "We'll be dried off soon."

Samantha blinked and put a hand over her throat as she turned to light the candle. Beginning to wonder if she should mention the uncanny figure she'd seen, she paused. Certainly, if someone had really walked through that door, her friends would have noticed. *Veronica's paranoia is finally getting to me*, she thought, pushing the notion away.

The four girls lined up in front of the locker room mirror, reflections of their shadowy faces smiling in the soft candlelight. "This is like one of those 'dead teenager' movies," Becca gasped sardonically. "Let's hope nothing's in here stalking us!"

"Don't say that," Samantha scolded in a coarse whisper. "We'll all ask for Jane at once and then repeat it at least ten times. I'll start and then all of you join in right away."

The others nodded.

"Jane?" Samantha said in a low voice as she gazed into the long mirror. The others chimed in almost simultaneously. "Jane?" they said, Becca and Lily smiling broadly as they intoned the ghost's name.

"Jane? Are you there, Jane? Please answer us," Samantha said.

By their twelfth attempt, her voice had grown pleading.

"Nothing going to happen. Let's go before we get caught," Becca said with some relief. She reached down for her gym bag and pulled out her jeans and t-shirt.

Just then, a gust of air passed over the flames of the melting candle, its fires dancing briefly. For a moment, Samantha could see the outline of a small, blurred shape coming into focus within the depths of the mirror.

A door slammed open outside in the pool room. The sound of a mop bucket on wheels being pushed over the tiled floor cut through the silence.

"It's Carl! Put out the light!" Becca said as she snuffed the candle's flames between her fingertips. Lily grabbed her clothes from the bench and wadded them into Becca's bag. This done, the two of them quickly slipped on their sneakers.

Becca dropped the spent candle into a plastic trash barrel. "There's an open window in here somewhere. I definitely felt a breeze when we first walked in."

Hurrying to the back of the dark locker room, Becca spied an open awning window above the sinks and toilet stalls. She waved the other girls over.

"Stand on me and then pull me up last," Becca whispered, half-enjoying the prospect of being caught. Ava nodded, clambered up Becca's braced body, and placed her feet on the taller girl's athletic shoulders. Panting, Ava slipped through the window, followed by Lily with Becca's gym bag, and then, lastly, Samantha.

The wheels of the mop cart had grown loud, and the door to the locker room abruptly flung open, bright light shining onto the rows of locker units. Lily and Samantha grabbed Becca's arms as she flailed desperately on the tips of her sneakers, and then pulled her roughly through the crevice under the window's pane.

They ran over the nighttime grounds of the school natatorium toward the parking lot. Breathing hard, the girls piled through the car's unlocked doors, Becca quickly starting the engine. In an instant, they were pulling out toward the lot's exit and the street beyond.

"That was close!" Becca shouted as they rode off, all smiles at their getaway. "But—admit it—it was loads of fun too! Just don't tell anyone—at least, not this semester."

Samantha looked out the backseat window of the sleek SUV as her friends talked and laughed, the late-night summer breeze blowing about her as they drove past tracts of suburban homes. *Did I really see something in the mirror?* Samantha worried, an uneasiness gripping her. *Or was it all just nerves?*

***

Placing a small stack of books on the library table in front of her, Samantha seated herself and took a deep breath, mentally preparing to dive into the volume at the top of the pile: *Urban Myths and Legends*, a hardcover book by some author she had never heard of. The books were mostly older, some several decades old, but these worn texts were all she'd been able to find in the local library's catalog database.

A quick Internet search earlier had revealed almost nothing about Creepy Jane except a few creepypastas, none of which identified

Creepy Jane by name. The books Samantha had pulled from the library shelves turned out to contain much more detail, but still made no mention of an urban legend centered around a dead girl called "Creepy Jane."

Over hours, Samantha read stories about some creature named the Slenderman; ghostly hitchhikers; black-eyed children (this one really scared her); an ax murderer dubbed "The Bunny Man"; and various tales of gateways to Hell hidden in abandoned buildings, hotel rooms, and other out-of-the-way places. But no Creepy Jane.

Had Veronica been telling the truth about making the story up, or had she lied to cover something up? Samantha sighed. She could never tell with Veronica. Like Becca said, that girl was a liar, and you never did know with her.

But something stood out in Samantha's memory of that night that continued to push her to question the events surrounding Miranda's death. As the police report recorded, there'd been no sign of forced entry and no unidentified fingerprints anywhere. The bathroom door had been locked from the inside. Each of these occurrences was hard to explain but, taken together, they were very strange indeed. There was something else too, half-buried in the back of Samantha's mind...

Officer Williams pressed his ear against the bathroom door a second time, hoping against hope that Miranda might answer him. After a moment, he reached into a heavy bag at his feet and removed a metal implement and a sledgehammer. His colleague, Officer Sanchez, stepped up and wedged the two-pronged fork at the implement's head between the door and its frame, then stepped aside as Officer Williams struck with the hammer. The sharp points of the head drove deep into the door's narrow gap, forming a wedge.

Both officers leveraged their weight against the entry tool's handle, prying the bathroom door open with a crack. Samantha rushed past the two men and stood over her sister; Miranda was sprawled on her back on the tile floor. Light from the hallway spilled over the dead body and glinted off a silver mirror lying face up next to the corpse. Samantha glanced down into the mirror's surface and saw someone staring back at her...

"Samantha, step away! Outside, now!" Officer Williams reached over and grabbed Samantha's arm, leading her out of the bathroom. "Stay with your mother," he said. When he returned, Officer Sanchez was checking Miranda for vital signs.

The events of that night jumbled together in Samantha's mind. At first, she'd dismissed what she had seen as a trick of the light, had convinced herself that the face was her own somehow distorted. But that face, it hadn't been a normal face—it was the face of someone evil...

Samantha's phone vibrated on the wood laminate table, pulling her attention back to the present moment. Mom was calling her, probably about the car. It was already early afternoon and Mom had wanted to do some shopping before the weekend. *I'll just let it go to voicemail,* Samantha thought absent-mindedly.

What if it's our house? A chill crept over Samantha. Pulling up a browser on her phone, she hurriedly searched records of their town's past for anything tragic. When nothing came up, she searched for her address. And before long, she found something.

More than half a century ago, another murder took place near the grounds of their new home, also involving a young girl. The girl had been strangled to death. The website mentioned the area surrounding their house had once been an apple orchard, with the house the only residence for several miles.

Olivia Radcliff was the murdered girl's name. She'd been the fourteen-year-old daughter of Helen Radcliff, a well-to-do widow. Mrs.

Radcliff regularly hired an immigrant named Giuseppe Rosini as a gardener and to pick apples in the orchard. Giuseppe spoke little English, and he was grateful for the work.

Mrs. Radcliff arrived home one summer afternoon to find Olivia missing. She searched the orchard and discovered Olivia among the rows of flowering apple trees, bleeding from her temple. There had been a struggle, and someone had strangled her until she died.

The police were quick to blame Mr. Rosini, who had neither an alibi nor the funds for a proper legal defense. An investigation into Mr. Rosini's past found he had attempted assault on a teenage girl in his home country before fleeing to avoid prosecution. The trial jury convicted him on only circumstantial evidence and Mr. Rosini was executed by hanging soon after.

Samantha slowly scrolled through the website's article and examined the embedded black and white photographs of Mrs. Radcliff and Olivia. Olivia was very beautiful—she wore a wide-brimmed straw hat and summer dress, her outstretched hand resting on the branch of an apple tree, but there was something quite disturbing about the picture itself.

The longer Samantha looked at the girl in the photo, the more she was taken by an unnatural coldness in the girl's aspect. Outwardly she was lovely, but there was something terribly cruel about the way she gazed back at the camera, or at whoever had taken that picture. Stranger still was Olivia's resemblance to herself; the girl could have been Samantha's long-lost sister from another era, the two were so similar in appearance.

***

"I'm so glad you called ahead. Visitor hours are almost done for today. But how did you find Mrs. Radcliff's address?" The young nurse led Samantha down a long hallway at the convalescent home, turning to smile at her intermittently.

"It wasn't hard," Samantha said. "Almost everyone's address is somewhere on the Internet if you know where to look." She glanced at her wristwatch: it was late afternoon. She had left her phone in the car as she was certain Mom would call her again.

"Mrs. Radcliff is our community's only centenarian; she's been here for I don't know how many years. You're the first guest she's had since I started here." The nurse stopped in the open doorway to the visitors' lounge and briefly gestured toward a very aged woman slouched in a wheelchair. The old woman looked down at the floor, seeming not to notice Samantha and the nurse's presence.

The nurse continued to speak in a quiet, almost sympathetic voice as the two watched Mrs. Radcliff from the doorway. "She's nearly blind now, just so you know, but she still has her faculties. You can visit with her here in the lounge. It'll be empty except for the two of you."

The nurse approached Mrs. Radcliff's wheelchair and leaned over to speak into her ear. "Mrs. Radcliff, this is your visitor, Samantha. She says she lives in your old house now with her mother."

Mrs. Radcliff looked up in Samantha's direction, her sightless eyes dull and opaque. "Yes? Samantha, please sit down in front of me so I can better hear you." Her voice still held some strength, even though her body was clearly failing.

"I hope you find out what you need for your summer project. I'll be back in thirty minutes." The nurse walked away casually, partially closing the door to the lounge behind her as she left.

The old woman wobbled her head as if trying to get her bearings before she spoke. "You live in my house on Rosewood Lane? Is that what you want to talk about?" Mrs. Radcliff seemed calm, but there was a hint of apprehension in her tone.

"Yes, there's a silver hand mirror my mother found in the attic. I think it may have belonged to your daughter, Olivia." Samantha studied Mrs. Radcliff's blotted and wrinkled face, thinking back to the photograph of her as a young woman.

Mrs. Radcliff continued to move her head back and forth but said nothing. After a long moment, she said, "Olivia? What do you know of my daughter?" Visibly agitated, a pallor of fear began to spread over the old woman's already ashen complexion.

"There's an image of a smiling girl wearing flowers in her hair on its back," Samantha explained. "Did you give that mirror to Olivia?"

"No," Mrs. Radcliff replied forcefully. "The mirror was mine when I was a girl, a gift from my own mother. Olivia would take it from my room and admire herself for hours. What a vain child she was."

Samantha waited a moment and then said, "I think Olivia may be trying to contact us from the afterlife." She leaned forward in the lounge chair after she spoke, waiting to hear Mrs. Radcliff's reaction to her claim about the supernatural.

Mrs. Radcliff again sat in silence, her head wobbling about. When she replied to Samantha, her raised voice was scalding, her words sharp and acerbic. "Olivia was born wicked. I could see the cruelty in her from early on, but her wickedness grew worse as she began to reach womanhood." Mrs. Radcliff's brow furrowed, as if she were in great pain.

"Animals would go missing from the neighbors' farms. Then, one day, a young boy vanished. Olivia said he had run away, but his body was later dredged up from the woods nearby. His body was...

"I found Olivia alone in the orchard. Her back was to me, standing among the trees not yet ready for the fall harvest. As she turned, she held something clenched in her hand.

"I stuck Olivia across the head with the butt of an ax. An ax I'd found in our shed, wrapped in rags, dried blood on its blade and on its handle.

"Olivia fell, and I knelt down to choke my daughter for what she had done. She fought. Oh, how she fought! Then, finally, her evil life was choked out of her."

Samantha sat motionless in the chair, stunned by this almost involuntary confession. Mrs. Radcliff gazed directly at Samantha, her thin brows arched, her milk-white eyes narrowing as if attempting to focus.

With a fierceness belying her frail appearance, Mrs. Radcliff suddenly reached forth with a bony hand and gripped Samantha's wrist, holding her fast. "But evil never truly dies," the old woman breathed. "Evil will always find a way to continue on, if it can."

The old woman closed her eyes under heavy lids and sank back into her wheelchair, exhausted. She released her grasp on Samantha's arm.

Samantha stood, eyes wide, and hurried away to find the nurse.

***

Samantha leaned against the open car door, rubbing her tender wrist. Her phone now showed two voicemail messages from Mom.

I'll listen to them while I'm driving back, Samantha thought contritely. *Mom must be pissed by now.*

As she pulled out of the parking lot, the first voicemail played from the phone's speakers. *"Hello, Sam, this is Mom. You're still not back from the library, so I'm going to step out with Veronica Peters' mother, Carol. She called me and said Veronica has serious insomnia, can't sleep. Carol thinks it has to do with Miranda, but Veronica won't say. Talk to you soon."*

Samantha deleted the first voicemail with her free hand as she drove and then let the second message play. *"Hello, Sam. This is Mom again. I hope you're OK. I'm back from coffee with Carol. She's really upset. She's afraid Veronica won't start college in a few weeks and doesn't know what to do. Carol also dropped by the police station with me on the way home and I picked up my mirror from evidence. Talk to you soon."*

Samantha took a deep breath and began to drive faster along the expressway. By the time she pulled into her driveway, the waning summer sun was setting below the horizon, casting long shadows from the nearby trees over their home.

The front door was unlocked. Samantha stepped into the silent house and closed the door behind her.

"Mom? Are you there?" Samantha called out. "I'm sorry I didn't call you back. I took another trip after the library."

She put her phone down on the kitchen table and looked around. "I really need to see that mirror you brought back with you," she called out again. "It's important."

Samantha turned the corner into the dim hallway, the last light of the day falling through the living room windows onto the rug. The bathroom door at the end of the hall was cracked open, a flickering light coming from inside the otherwise dark space.

Samantha stopped. "Mom?"

The bathroom door swung open and Sharon hurtled from the darkness, grabbing Samantha by the throat. Mother and daughter tumbled onto the hardwood floor, Sharon's icy cold hands violently clutching Samantha in a vise-like grip. Her eyes bulging with madness,

Sharon tightened her stranglehold, a manic, gape-mouthed grin on her face.

Pinned on her back, Samantha's mouth fell open as she struggled to swallow one more breath. The image of her mother above her, hands around her throat, grew blurry as darkness closed in...

"Hello, there's a medical emergency at 1211 Rosewood Lane. My mother's had a heart attack. No, she's not responding to me. I'm sorry, I can't tell. Please send an ambulance."

Samantha put her phone down on the kitchen table. She stepped over Sharon's body in the hallway and walked into the bathroom, flipping on the light switch. The silver mirror lay on the bathroom rug, its glass surface unmarred and intact.

Samantha touched the mirror fondly and then admired her own reflection, tucking a loose lock of blonde hair behind an ear. Then, wrapping the antique piece in its white linen cloth, she placed it at the bottom of the dresser drawer for safekeeping.

About the Author

James Dermond is a writer who lives in Colorado. Intrigued from a very young age by horror anthologies and the short story form, this book is his latest modest contribution to the genre.

Doorways to the Unseen 6: 6 Tales of Terror and Suspense is the sixth volume in a series of short story collections. The seventh volume in the series will be published in October 2023.

To sign up for free eBooks and other future giveaways, please subscribe to James Dermond's author website here:

www.jamesdermond.com

James Dermond's Amazon Author Page

https://www.amazon.com/James-Dermond/e/B01M1S54YP

James Dermond's Goodreads Author Page

https://www.goodreads.com/author/show/15862747.James_Dermond

James Dermond on Facebook

https://www.facebook.com/JamesDermondAuthor/

James Dermond on Twitter

https://twitter.com/JamesDermond

Postscript

The hank you for reading this latest volume in the short horror story series, Doorways to the Unseen! We are now on volume six of what will eventually become a twelve-volume series of books. The planned publication schedule is two volumes in 2023 and then for the next two years, with the final volume released in April 2026. A multi-volume hardcover edition of the collected stories would then be released in October of the same year.

If you enjoyed this collection of stories, please leave a review on Amazon and other online bookstores where volumes in the Doorways to the Unseen series can be found. A positive review will help promote the book and inform other readers of the book's merits.